CHRISTINA D. AMBROSE

Haunted Souls

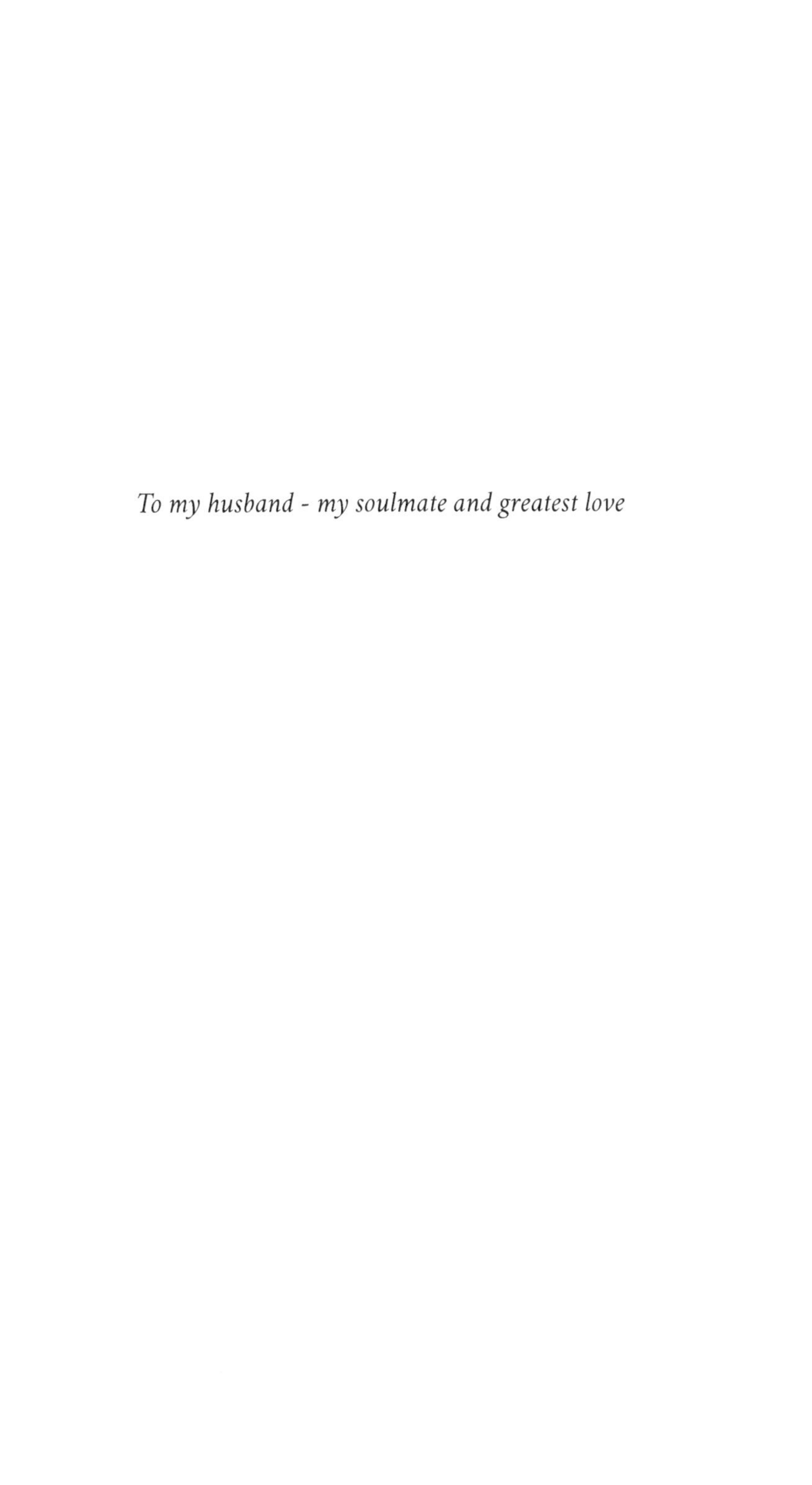

To my husband - my soulmate and greatest love

Contents

1

Whispers in the Dark

Something slipped into Abigail Huxley's sleeping mind. A passing thought of darkness, drifting unperceived–yet lingering, festering, deep in her mind. Like a whisper of promises broken in her heart.

A familiar presence fell within the space between dreams and reality, and the night held its breath until a whisper breathed into her ear.

A call to her.

Silent–yet her body responded as if it were a roar.

She bolted upright in her bed, panting, her hand pressed over her aching heart, her eyes wide with panic, waiting. A salty ocean breeze from the open window moved the curtains, and there it was. That beckoning voice again.

She had thought it had been her imagination those many months ago when they told her that her beloved had died, lost at sea. Or had it been years now?

The memory of his voice lingered at the edges of her mind as sleep tried to lull her again. Could it be in dreams where she heard that sweet timbre, or felt the softness of his blonde hair? How the roughness of his stubble scratched her delicate skin as he kissed her cheek? Yes, it had been a dream, cruel and heartbreaking.

Her breath caught when she heard it again, so faint that she could barely perceive it. Her heart ached at the sound. It wasn't possible, but there was no other explanation.

"Abby," the voice breathed, and a chill raced up her spine.

It was there, faint yet true–a voice from her past. One that had haunted her every moment, waking and asleep.

William.

Her beloved.

Her intended.

She dashed to the window and gazed out into the moonlit night. The waves rolled quietly onto the shoreline below, and the sound found its way to Abby tucked inside her small house on a tall cliff overlooking the ocean.

The quaint cottage was supposed to be their home. William had built it for them before he set out that fateful day. They were prepared to marry the next month. But that now seemed so long ago–a memory lost to time. A memory that she clung to, just as she clung to the hope that one day he would return.

As time rolled on, her hope faded, and she forced herself to look to the future. Many years had passed, and Frederick, a man from town, courted her. He bided his time, lingering by her side as she mended her broken heart, waiting patiently until Abby finally accepted his proposal. He wasn't a stranger but a dear friend of William's that Abigail could trust. His smiles, however, were guarded, and his gestures were calculating – unlike William, whose smiles were warm and friendly and whose words were kind and thoughtful. This friend was nowhere near the man that William was, but she had little choice. Frederick and Abby were set to marry in a fortnight, and the guilt of betrayal ate at her heart.

Before Abby knew what was happening, her feet led her to the doorway and out onto the cliffs overlooking the sea. The cold breeze blew her curly auburn hair and chemise as she tried to listen for the sound again, her heart squeezing in her chest. Icy fingers of salty air penetrated her skin, stealing the last of her warmth.

The night was deathly silent except for the roll of waves. Her toes curled into the sand and grasses. Not a single fowl or insect made a sound as she stood there, her breath shallow. The moon cast an eerie glow on the water and shore below, and her chemise and skin took on an unearthly luminosity, making her believe this moment was more dream than reality.

"Abby."

The whisper rang through her soul, stealing her breath. Her eyes swept the shoreline, trying to find the source of her unease. Wisps of frosty air gathered, forming a mist that Abby had never seen before. Where there had been hope, fear now replaced it, for surely what she saw was unnatural and otherworldly. Abby's mind wanted her to run back into the cottage, but her body disobeyed, frozen as she watched the mist crawl toward the cliff, up the steep face, to rest beside her. Her breath was shaky as she watched the ethereal, indefinable curtain thicken and solidify, then darken to form a shape that she never thought she'd see again.

When the fog dissipated, an apparition of a man that Abby had longed to touch again stood before her, unaltered by time, just like she'd last seen him before he had been taken from her those ten years hence.

"Abby," he murmured as his deep voice rumbled in his chest.

He touched her face, the caress like the cool embrace of the sea. He smelled of brine, driftwood, and seaweed as she walked along the shoreline, waiting for his return as if the sea's essence penetrated every cell of his skin.

Abby wanted to scream, but her voice was trapped in her throat. This *couldn't* be him - her beloved William, the man who brightened her world so long ago with his warm smiles and kind words.

Yet, it seemed he stood here before her in the moonlight.

He cupped Abby's jaw with his hands and tilted her face up to gaze into his eyes which seemed to glow a warm brown even in the darkness of night. His face descended onto hers, and their lips met, cold and clammy as if death himself was kissing her. The kiss ignited something in Abby's body, a warmth that seeped into every limb, to every finger and toe, to every strand of her hair. It electrified her entire being, and when he broke away, she mourned the loss of it.

The wind whipped up the cliffs again, mussing their hair along with his shirt and her gown.

He was *real.* A smile spread across her face as she gazed at his loving eyes. But the warmth of his eyes faded, replaced with anger.

"You disappoint me." His voice was firm and full of regret.

Abby was confused. "Dearest William, what have I done?"

"You forgot that you are mine!"

His anger crashed into her like a great wave, and she felt herself being pulled under. She gasped and fell into the darkness that overtook her.

2

Broken Promises

Abby awoke nestled in her sheets and blankets. The soft morning sunlight streamed in through her open window. She glanced around the room in a panic. Everything seemed to be in place. The door to her cottage was closed, and the bolt was latched firmly. She recalled wandering out to the edge of the cliff last night, but nothing afterward. How had she returned to her bed?

Visions filled her mind. William had been there with her on the cliff. But that was impossible. He had been assumed dead for ten years. His body was lost to the sea if the men on board were to be believed. Something deep inside her hoped they had been wrong, praying that William had found his way to some distant shore and was trying to get back to her.

The apparition that appeared that night was not alive or human. How could it ever be genuine, what her eyes had seen that night? Abby knew that ghosts were unspoken fears of loss and things left undone. Words undeclared. Imagined figures of a distracted mind.

It had to have been a dream. Nothing more. Any other answer

would destroy her.

Abby had dreamt of him many nights, more than she could ever count. Primarily in those nightly visions, Will was working on the house, building furniture or the stone wall, or thatching the roof. He talked to her while she assisted him in his endeavors. Showed her how to hold the chisel and hammer just right to make the perfect cut on wood.

But the other times, her dreams filled with an intimacy she had almost forgotten. His gentle voice. The soft touch of his hand brushing against hers. And his kisses. The thing that hurt the worst was each time she woke, memories of him slipped away, fleeting until she couldn't remember the timbre of his voice. How he smiled. The sound of his laugh.

Time had stolen him from her just like the sea had.

The song of birds drew her to the window, and Abby ambled to the opening, frightened of what she might find, her feet slow on the chill of the stone floor. The sight that met her was like any other day – the cows grazed by the stones next to the cottage. The sun had already burned off the morning mist. It was a typical day on the cliff, and yet she couldn't ease the ache in her heart, the empty space that had lingered since the day William disappeared in the cold, cruel waves.

Her hand covered her racing heart. She couldn't bear the sight of the merciless waves. Stepping away from the window, she leaned against the firm bedpost. Her hand brushed the smoothness of the wood, and she remembered the care William's hands took to shape it. The smile he gave her as he spoke his dreams of their wedding night and longed to see her laid out across the bed he made.

Abby felt the blush as it heated her face at such memories. These reminiscences were not for her to linger on now that he was gone. They were only broken promises that would never come to pass. She shoved idle thoughts of the past away, changed into her chemise, and donned her corset for the day. Next came wool stockings and petticoats, then her green wool skirt, white blouse, and white apron. Finally, her leather shoes and shawl. Abby tamed her long unruly red hair into a low bun.

She had long been the gossip of wagging tongues, heiress to a fortune and home inherited from a man she never married. The words and stares bothered her, but she knew the vile whispers were false. Abby and Will had never consummated their love. She had only known tantalizing promises and sweet kisses from a man who held her honor in the highest esteem. She had been just as shocked as the rest of the town when William's last will and testament had been read.

Only her uncle, her brother, and a few friends encouraged her to hold her head high. William's friend Edward and his wife, Sarah, had stood by her. His other companion, Frederick, took her arm to lead her into the heart of the church each Sunday and defended her honor when anyone ever questioned it.

Abby shoved a small log into the woodstove and struck the flint to set it aflame before closing the metal door on the stove with a clang. Life trudged on, and time wouldn't stand still for her. Breakfast needed to be made, water fetched, and animals fed. Her daily obligations beckoned.

She left the stove to heat and took the pail to the well to collect water for the day. Walking across a small piece of land behind the house, she reached the well, uncovering it to attach the pail to the hook. The fall air was crisp in the morning light, and Abby enjoyed the changes of colors in the leaves and land.

As she lowered the pail, Abby watched the cows eat peacefully. This was the life she was supposed to have with William, or as she lovingly called him, Will. He helped shape this peaceful life with his hands, sweat, and blood for the future. He would have gladly called her "*wife.*"

"*One more week at sea, Abby,*" he had said. *Just to get the money I need for my shop.*"

Books. Pens. Ink and parchment, paper and journals: these were the supplies he would stock, in a store for those who could afford the small niceties with their bonuses. For those who could not write, Will would offer his penmanship services.

A safe, honest living far from the dark and turbulent sea.

It frightened Abby each time he climbed aboard the boat and sailed beyond the familiar shores of home. She had counted down the days to his final departure when he would climb on board that fishing vessel for the last time. Each day a step closer to him walking away from the ocean.

On the last day, Will smiled at Abby and kissed her sweetly for all to see on the docks, promising that all would be well when he returned. He spoke of his excitement about their coming nuptials and whispered in her ear how much he couldn't wait to… *fuck* her. She scolded him for his bawdy language, but secretly preened at his words. With one final kiss, he boarded the boat, a man full of life, dreams, and hopes for the future.

But a few days after he left her, those on shore could see the vicious nature of a terrible storm as the waves tossed and lightning struck. Abby worried. She sobbed. She hoped despite the pit in her stomach. As the hours and days dragged on, fear faded into reality. Abby's life changed when the ship returned battered and beaten, sails torn–and missing men. Her Will was gone, taken by the ocean he longed to leave.

Abby wiped a tear from her cheek as she detached the full pail from the rope. She never knew true pain until Frederick told her of the wave that dragged her love to the depths below. Even after Frederick recounted the horror of that day, she refused to believe he was gone. She prayed, wished, and bargained with God and all spirits of the deep for Will's return. Day after day, she walked the shores awaiting his return for ten long years.

But it was never enough.

Abby returned to the house, pail in hand, setting it on the table by the stove. She grabbed an iron pot, its heavy weight clanging against the stovetop. A handful of oats and the last of the cream went into the pot, along with a partial cup of water. Abby stirred it a moment before heading out to check on the cows.

The cliffs called to her as the dream stirred in her mind again–the feel of Will's lips on hers. His eyes watching her.

The waves broke onto shore as gulls cried from above. Abby spied a fishing ship on the horizon, making its way out to sea. A breeze caught her skirts, and she felt a strange pull on her soul.

"Abby."

She gasped as she looked behind her to search for the owner of the faint voice. The curtain inside her window fluttered, pulling her gaze from the cows, but there was nothing.

No. A trick of the mind.

Abby pulled her shawl closer to her body and stormed into her house. Her porridge was bubbling. How long had she been out there?

She grabbed the pot handle with her apron and skirt, placing it off the side to cover the burner. After spooning the meager amount into a bowl, she ate quickly. She was already late getting to the docks, and Frederick was an impatient man, valuing timeliness and carefulness above all. Abby huffed a bitter laugh, for she was anything but those qualities, adding to her loathing over why she agreed to finally marry him after his asking all these years.

She needed to leave thoughts of Will in the past.

But the frightening vision the night before knocked Abby's sureness a-kilter, making her doubt all that she knew. Distracted as she was, Abby left the house without noticing the large wet footprints leading from the door to her bed.

Footprints that left no trail back the other way.

3

Disillusioned Expectations

bby latched her front door before making her way carefully down the narrow path of the cliffs toward town. She adjusted her shawl on her shoulders as an icy breeze wrapped around her, and felt a tug on the hem of her skirt as it caught on a batch of scrub brush. The jerk knocked her off balance, sending her skidding onto her knees and hands. She tumbled into the pebbles and brush lining the path until she landed at the edge of the cliff, staring at the rocks far below with rough waves crashing onto them. Her heart thundered in her chest as she righted herself, brushing the dust of the footpath off her skirt and noting trivial scratches on her palms.

Death would be an easy path if she tumbled over the cliff. She scolded herself for her carelessness while collecting her thoughts. Abby couldn't afford to be distracted. She was already late for her meeting with Frederick.

By the time Abby made it to town, the early morning boats had arrived, with crews unloading their bounty from the sea. Horse and cart passed her on the main road as the bustle of the quaint English town filled her senses.

The time she spent living with her uncle within the heart of the small village had opened Abby's eyes to her distaste for residing too close to one's neighbors. The noise and smell had been part of the reason William had built their cottage on the cliff, and Abby couldn't have agreed more with him. They both preferred the fresh sea air and the sounds of the ocean to the man-made ruckus of living within the settlement.

Abby had come to live in this town just after her uncle's wife had passed on. He was the eldest brother of her father's family and seventeen years his senior. Uncle Ulysses Huxley had declared himself too old and impatient to take on another wife and, being childless, had requested her father to allow one of his nieces to manage his household. Abby, or Abigail, as was her birth name, had been sixteen at the time, and her older brother, Sebastian, had been tasked to bring her to Robin Hood's Bay.

Abby had never seen the sea in all its infinite glory – the everchanging mystical world that gave and took away. She met William that first day at the fish market while he was unloading large woven baskets of fish from the boat he had disembarked. Will told her that she had caught his eye with her pretty embroidered shawl and auburn hair that refused to stay in her bun. He had sworn that day to his friend, Frederick, that he would wed Abby one day.

Will courted Abby for almost two years before Uncle Huxley allowed them to become engaged. Her uncle had acted as her guardian at the request of her father, for he had become homebound from an old back injury, and agreed that Uncle Huxley would be a better judge of Will's character and intentions toward Abby.

The memories of those happy moments brought a painful

sadness to mind. As Abby tried to hold back the tears, she felt a brush on her shoulder, like a comforting gesture. Startled, she glanced around to see who had touched her, only to find no one nearby. The sensation set her uneasy as she continued down the path past stores, pubs, and liveries toward the docks.

As her boots hit the wood planks, Abby spied the familiar face of Frederick, his hair dark and wavy, skin sun-kissed as he directed the delivery of fish-ladened baskets. When Frederick saw her, a smile spread across his handsome face.

"There you are," he sighed in relief. "I was wondering where you were."

Abby blushed as he brushed a stray lock of hair from her face. "I got a late start this morning." She glanced around the docks at the people coming and going. "What can I do to help?"

The look on Frederick's face softened. "You know you don't have to help, Abby. Will left enough money for you, so you don't have to work. Besides," he stepped closer to her, "we'll be married soon."

Frederick reached out to take her hand, and Abby grabbed onto her shawl to avoid his touch. It still felt wrong to be touched by him. Her heart remained haunted by the embraces and kisses Will used to give her. Having another man touch her was awkward and unwanted, but it was something she was going to have to accept. Frederick was going to be her husband soon.

"I know you don't need my help, but I wish to have something to do."

"Well, if you lived in town, you would be closer to people. You would have more opportunities to participate in society."

Abby scrunched her nose. "You know how I dislike the smells and the noise."

Frederick laughed. "Yes, well. Let's see what you can do, shall we?"

She nodded, and Frederick placed his hand gently on her lower back as he guided her through the crowd. A sensation radiated from the base of her spine, making her feel off balance. Her legs wobbled, and she fell away from Frederick, landing on the ground. Abby turned to gaze up at Frederick crossly, for it felt like someone had pushed her. But the look on his face told another story - one of concern.

"Are you well? Did you trip?" Frederick asked as he helped her stand.

Abby brushed down her skirt, making sure everything was in place. "Yes, I think I am. I must have caught my foot on something."

Even though she said the words, Abby knew them to be untrue. It had definitely been a push of some sort that had landed her on the ground. A shove that seemed to come from the small of her back. As Frederick tried to touch her again, Abby pulled away, hugging her arms around her abdomen to still the swirl of emotion there. She glanced around, looking for an understanding of what had happened.

"Abigail, are you sure you are well? You seem pale. Are you ill? You're acting very strangely today," Frederick said quietly, and he drew close to her again. He touched her forehead with the back of his hand, testing her warmth.

"Well, I didn't sleep well, I suppose," Abby muttered as his hand cupped her face. "The anniversary of Will's death is a few days away, and you know how it affects me."

The softness of Frederick's face hardened as he pulled away and brushed a hand through his hair. Abby's breath caught in her throat as she saw the quiet anger burn in his eyes at the mention of Will's name. She hadn't meant to speak of him, but his name slipped so easily from her lips.

"Yes, I do." Frederick studied her for a moment. "Abigail, I have tried to be patient with you. I gave you time to mourn your former betrothed. Ten years to mourn him, in fact; a very generous offer I bestowed on you. But he was not your husband. He never was. I, on the other hand, will be your husband, and I expect you to put the past behind you, so we can truly start anew."

"Yes," Abby almost growled at his cruel words. "How noble of you to make such a sacrifice for the fiancée of your dead friend, a man who was like a *brother* to you." She looked firmly into his dark eyes. "I can't tell my heart to stop loving him like one can snuff out a candle. Time has eased the pain but not erased it. And as for what my duties will be when I become your wife? I know them well. You have reminded me often enough since our engagement. You may be entitled to own my body and possessions, but you will not be master of my mind or thoughts. Take care to remember that."

Frederick's face darkened before he looked at the people surrounding them, checking to see if any had overheard her. His jealousy of a dead man was so clear on his face. He grabbed her arm and roughly pulled her under one of the sorting tents. Empty baskets lay in all kinds of positions, and the table had remnants of fish blood, guts, and scales. The smell of it all invaded Abby's nose as she tried to pull away from his grasp.

"William may have tolerated that sharp tongue of yours, but I will not have you humiliate me in front of my peers. You will listen to me: when we marry, you will move into town. You will attend the social occasions required of a woman of the station into which you are marrying. And I will sell that god-forsaken house on the cliff that you so fiercely cling to. Or better yet, I'll tear it down myself, stone by stone, so that I rip any reminder of him away from you. Then maybe, you will be the wife you need to be."

"You wouldn't dare!" she snarled.

"I shall."

"Then I will not marry you."

"I have paid my bride price to your family, and all the documents have been signed. You will be mine willingly or otherwise, lest you be ruined for any other offers of marriage."

Abby blinked back the tears in her eyes, gasping. She understood his threat and the weight it held for her future. She knew Frederick to be a fair man. When people were kind to him, he returned the sentiment. If people crossed him, he treated them likewise. Frederick held power in Robin Hood's Bay. He owned several of the ships that employed the fishermen. The fish they brought in gave the town wealth and prosperity.

Abby remembered the kind, funny young man Frederick used to be when Will worked on Frederick's father's boat. They would walk together through the meadows near the bog. Life was full of laughter and happiness until Will began officially courting Abby. Frederick turned melancholy, yet Will paid no heed to Abby's observations of his friend's change of mood.

Now, Frederick was a man possessive of the fact Abby had agreed to be his wife. She wished her uncle was still alive to see the cruelty of Frederick's actions and insist the engagement must end. But wishing wasn't going to help the situation., and part of her must admit, Frederick was right about the past. Sometimes the thoughts of the dead needed to be buried, for those thoughts could haunt the living.

And Abby felt haunted.

An unearthly warmth lingered on her cheek as the tears fell. "You are right," Abby said plainly. "The past needs to remain so."

Frederick sighed significantly before caressing her cheek to wipe the tears away. "All will be better when we take our vows. I promise." He hooked his finger under her chin to raise it to meet her eyes. "I only want what is best for you, Abigail. I truly do. Please believe me."

Abby gazed into his eyes and, upon seeing the softness there, nodded. Frederick pressed his lips to her forehead, Abby knowing this was an apology for his uncivilized behavior.

"The next boat should be in soon, and I must give directions. But if you want to remain, we could share something to eat together." Frederick's voice went soft and tender again. He was the old Frederick Abby had known so well. "I heard the meat pies at Nellie's are delicious today. Something about new spices that she got delivered from France."

Abby gave him a weak smile. "That would be nice." She glanced around the tent. "Meanwhile, I will clean this station, so people can have a place to work."

Frederick nodded. "Good girl. I knew I could count on you. I will be back soon to fetch you."

Abby nodded, and he smiled at her before he left the tent.

She sighed heavily as she rolled up her sleeves and hung her shawl in a clean area. A bucket of brackish water was easy to fetch, and she found a scrub brush near one of the tables. As she cleaned, Abby knew that her lot in life was one she wished she could change. She had heard of fathers or guardians that allowed their daughters to back out of their weddings, but she knew her father had already used the bride's price that Frederick had given him. It was gone.

Items for her trousseau chest had been bought and prepared for her – lovely dresses, shoes, hats, and jewelry fitting for someone of her station. All the niceties expected for Abby to have on her wedding day, except for the gown she was planning to wear for the nuptials–the wedding dress Will had commissioned to be made for her. She was going to wear it in memory of her beloved, and thanked the heavens that Frederick had never seen the gown. What he didn't know wouldn't hurt him.

There was the softest of sounds, and Abby stopped the scrub of the brush to glance around. She thought she heard her name - the faintest of whispers. But there was no one nearby. Shrugging off the sensation of unease, she blamed the bristles of the brush in her hand and, pushing the suspicion from her mind, continued her work.

She had to steel herself for the rest of the day with a smile on her face, shoving the guilt away so it wouldn't consume her.

4

The Ties that Bind

Sharing a meal with Frederick turned out to be a mistake. He was still in a sour mood with her from earlier, but Abby tried to engage in conversation with him.

"If I may be so bold," Abby began under the scrutiny of Frederick's ire, "I am looking forward to maintaining a household again. It's been so long since I have had to coordinate deliveries and social events."

Frederick's face brightened at the subject of the conversation. "Yes, it has. You used to run Mr. Huxley's household when you first moved here."

Abby nodded as she finished her savory piece of pie. Frederick had been right - the pies today were incredibly delicious. "Yes, my uncle loved to entertain, even at his age, though it was mostly to play cards with his friends. Also, I arranged deliveries for his business at the warehouse. Supplies and such."

Frederick frowned. "The day Ulysses passed was a sad day. He provided an invaluable service for this town. Luckily, I had enough saved to purchase the warehouse to keep it running."

Abby remembered those weeks. It was only a few months prior, and she had stepped in to assist her brother, Sebastian, with her uncle's affairs. He had been sent as a legal representative on their father's behalf. They began by selling off the assets and the house. Abby had not been surprised when Frederick stepped forward to inquire about purchasing the warehouse and distribution rights for overseas goods.

"Abby, how are you holding up?"

Abby looked to find her brother's clear blue eyes gazing at her with concern. She was still getting used to the idea of Sebastian being here with her after only conversing with him in letters for so long.

"I am well, Brother. Uncle was a bit of a curmudgeon, but he looked kindly after me."

Every word was genuine, even though Uncle Huxley had been a hard, gruff man. He had seen to Abby's best interest. He had, after all, championed her betrothal to Will after her father had initially expressed his disapproval. In the years following Will's disappearance and presumed death, Ulysses watched over her, ensuring she had attended important events and church services.

Sebastian sighed as he brushed a hand through his disheveled hair. "I know you were fond of our uncle, but I am speaking of William Johnson. It has been nine years since his death."

Abby felt tears prick at the corners of her eyes. "Disappeared. I refuse to believe that he is truly gone. He promised me, Sebastian, he would come back."

Her fingers touched the crystal decanter on the table, noting the curve and cut of the glass while trying to distract herself from all the feelings welling up inside before she allowed those wretched tears to burst forth. Sebastian gathered up in his arms as she cried. She cursed her broken heart for this hollow feeling inside.

Damn these tears. *They made Abby seem weak and fragile.*

"There, there, my sweet Abigail. I know he did, and I am sure he would have returned if it were within his power. But Abby, you have to look forward to the future. William's money will only last for so long."

"I work to add money to my purse."

"Yes, I know," Sebastian pulled back to look her in the eyes. "But Abby, your coffers are being depleted each year. You are unable to get enough work to balance your deficit. Within a few years, you will be destitute. You need to make plans to wed again."

A deep-seated horror surged through her body. "Marry? I cannot."

He cupped her face gently. "Abby, you must. Either that or you are welcome to move to London with my family and me. We have an extra room since Alexa married."

Abby had remembered her niece's wedding fondly. "I cannot leave, Sebastian."

Sebastian stood and massaged the back of his neck as he paced before turning back to her. "I didn't want to bring it up so soon, but maybe this news would change your mind. Someone has approached me to negotiate your hand in marriage. I have sent word to Father about it."

Abby didn't know why she felt betrayed at the idea. For a moment, she stared at the floor, at a loss for words.

Her voice was barely a whisper as she pushed the words out of her throat, where they wished to stay. "Who is it?"

"Frederick Evans."

Abby's eyes flicked up to meet Sebastian's. "Frederick has asked for a marriage contract?"

The words felt foreign on her tongue. Frederick had been there for her since the day Will disappeared. He had held her hand when she cried. He walked the beach with her to look out on the horizon, and attended church with her to keep her company. He had been her constant friend since that horrible day.

Sebastian nodded as he sat next to her again. "From your letters, he has been a constant companion these past nine years, a friend who has helped you stay sane through your mourning. I couldn't see a better man to take care of you and be your loyal husband." He shifted to take her hands. "Abby. Sweet Abigail, I beg you to consider his proposal. He cares for you as I do."

Abby couldn't help the tear that fell down her cheek. "I will consider it."

Sebastian smiled broadly at her. "Good." He patted her hands. "Good."

Her brother had only wanted the best for her, but no one could have guessed the possessive nature of Frederick Evans. Abby had not seen it until she agreed to wed him. If any man, dead or alive, dared come near her or into her thoughts, he stormed and raged enviously. She had dared not broach the subject with her brother when he had so much responsibility on his hands dealing with their father's failing estate.

Pushing her meat pie around her plate, Abby glanced up to watch Frederick as he waxed poetic about what a fine man her uncle had been. She gripped her fork so hard that her knuckles turned white.

Frederick's eyes lingered on her in silence before she realized his attention. "Abigail, are you sure you are well?"

Abby roughly set down her fork. "No, I fear I am not." She stood suddenly. "I need to go home and rest."

Frederick tensed as he stood with her. "Then I shall accompany you."

She knew she needed to change tactics, or he would follow as she made her way home. Frederick was a vain man when it came to his importance within the village, so Abby planned to use it to distract him and stroke his ego. She prayed her deception would work, freeing her of his presence.

"No, no, Frederick. You are a busy man, and I wish not to take you from your duties. Forgive me."

Frederick studied her. "If you are sure?"

Abby nodded, and Frederick relaxed as he took her hand to kiss her palm tenderly. "I hope you feel better, my love."

Her stomach threatened to upheave. She didn't understand what was going on. Maybe she was still spooked after last night's dream. Or perhaps she realized the horrible mistake in which she had cornered herself.

Abby bade Frederick farewell and headed out into the late afternoon air. Something about the atmosphere made her feel like the world was closing in on her. Perhaps it was the situation, or perchance it was because she felt watched by unseen eyes. A shiver shot up her spine as she glanced around the uncrowded street. People hurried on with their tasks, and yet Abby couldn't shake a feeling in her bones; an uneasiness that plagued her.

She stopped at the butcher to purchase scraps of meat for a stew she wanted to prepare that evening and for a small loaf of bread at the bakery. As she strolled through town toward the cliff path to home, she noticed a new store occupying one of the buildings.

A building she recognized from many years ago

The place where Will wished to open his store.

Various people had used the building over the years. It had been a tailor shop for many years until the tailor moved to the next town over due to the railroad opening. There had been a millinery shop where Abby had worked for a time. But now, Abby was curious about this new shop. Stalks of dried herbs hung in the window along with colorful bottles and various jars displayed for passersby - an apothecary.

Abby had never seen one in town. She had heard of them at the more important ports like Whitby down the coast, where the town physician would procure special medicines unavailable here. Of course, Abby didn't typically come this way because of the memories it stirred up.

The bell rang as she entered the shop, and Abby was bombarded with all sorts of aromas. The air was warm, and there was a tinge of smoke from pungent-smelling herb being burned in a bowl. The little shop was unassuming from the outside, but within it lay a visual treasure trove. Jars and pots of various sizes and colors lined the shelves, each one filled with different dried plants, powders, or liquids. Dried herbs hung from hooks on the ceiling.

Being back in the room brought back sweet memories of Will, and she thought back fondly of the excitement he had when he showed her the space.

"And here will be shelves displaying the different fountain pens and tips," Will said with a contagious grin. *"Oh, Abby. I have put in the final order with your uncle, and he said the rest should be here within a fortnight."*

Abby glanced around the space and remembered all that Will had mapped out. Boxes still unpacked spread throughout the room. And Will. It was beautiful to see his eyes lit with such excitement.

"It's all so wonderful, Will."

He pulled her into his arms. "And it is ours, Abby. No more going to sea for me, and you will be my wife." He couldn't contain the chuckle that came from him. "And we will have twelve children."

Abby laughed. "Twelve? Sir, you have great expectations from me."

Will's face softened with such warmth and adoration. "I want to fill our home with love."

He gave her a quick kiss on the forehead before taking her hand, then pulled her into a closed dance position to waltz with her. Abby giggled as they danced in the room. Happiness burst forth through her heart. Will made her more whole than she had ever felt.

She didn't know how long they danced in each other's arms, for time seemed to slow to allow them to enjoy the moment. Will stopped to gaze into her eyes as his gentle hand cupped her face.

"Please, Abby," Will beseeched.

Abby rolled her eyes at his pleading gaze. "Well, I'm not going to be the one who has to add rooms onto our house."

His smile beamed as his lips descended on hers with a bruising kiss.

"Can I help you?" a woman's voice called from behind her.

Abby turned with a gasp at the interruption. A short, older woman stood there waiting for an answer. Abby gazed around the room and realized she had been lost in a dream—a beautiful reverie that she had once lived, here in this very room.

Tears threatened to fall. Abby touched her lips and swore she could feel the ghost of his kiss still on them.

The words on Abby's lips hesitated. What could she say that would make this less strange? *Stick to the truth.*

"I have difficulty sleeping. Strange dreams. Do you have something that could help with that?"

The older woman adjusted her spectacles to look at her better, studying her intently.

"Strange dreams, you say?" the woman asked, her voice rough with age, as she made her way behind the counter. "I'm Myrtle Ravenwood, by the way, but you may call me Myrtle. I haven't seen you before in town." She pulled a few bowls and bottles from a hidden shelf.

"Yes, strange dreams," Abby answered as she followed her. "I tend to stay near the docks. I live in a cottage on the cliff."

Another young girl appeared next to Myrtle. The girl flicked her bound, black hair over her shoulder as she curtsied and smiled at Abby.

"This is my apprentice, Emily," Myrtle gestured toward the girl before she began to combine several ingredients. "And your name?"

"It's Abigail Huxley."

Myrtle stopped combining ingredients to study Abby. "Abigail Huxley as in William Johnson's betrothed?"

Abby stepped back. She had a strong instinct to run, but her legs didn't want to move. "Yes."

It was a simple word, but it seemed so hard for her to say.

Myrtle stared for a moment before nodding. "I knew him when he was a boy," she said sadly. "I was sorrowful to hear that he had passed. Good lad."

Abby watched as the woman worked her gnarled hands, mixing the paste in the bowl before her.

"So, in these strange visions, do you feel frightened?"

The question startled Abby. She looked between the two women who seemed to be waiting on her answer with great curiosity.

"Yes."

"Are you able to move?"

Abby thought about the dream before she answered. "No. I cannot."

Myrtle nodded as she continued to mix, adding pinches of some herb or another. "Do you have a sense of lost time?"

"Really, I don't understand what this has to do with a strange dream that is keeping me from sleep." Abby couldn't hide the frustration in her tone. She wanted to pick up her skirts and leave, but yet, there she stood.

When the paste was finished, Myrtle handed the bowl to Emily to place its contents inside a tiny pouch.

"Miss Abigail. I must be honest. I feel something surrounding you. A darkness. And this dream? I believe it to be more." Myrtle shifted to glance at Emily, who turned to study Abby. "Do you see it, Emily?"

The girl narrowed her eyes before tilting her head to the side. "I see it, too. Possession?"

Myrtle shook her head. "No, I fear something darker."

Emily glanced back at Abby before tying the pouch closed. "Yes, I see it. Do you think this will work?"

Myrtle hummed. "If she wears it all the time. Can you do that for me, Miss Abigail?"

Abby stared between the two women. What they were saying was impossible, let alone lacking any sanity. She shook her head. "I don't understand."

Myrtle handed her the pouch necklace. It weighed so little in her hand, but it felt powerful as she stood in the presence of these women.

"Something is coming for you. There has been an awakening. This magic charm, if worn, should help protect you."

Fear gripped Abby's heart. "An awakening? Something coming for me? What do you mean? Am I in danger?"

Myrtle tsked as she made her way to Abby. "So many questions that I don't have answers for. But something is very clear; you must be cautious. Wear the charm." Her gnarled hand covered the charm sitting in Abby's hand. "Promise me."

The older woman's pleading felt sincere, and Abby couldn't

help but feel that she should agree.

"I will."

Myrtle smiled at her. "Good girl. Now off with you. The day grows dark, and if you live on the cliffs, you will need all the light you can get to navigate home."

"How much do I owe you?"

"Nothing. A token gift for the woman who brought so much light into William's life."

It seemed wrong to leave without giving a payment for the charm, but Abby nodded before thanking them and hurrying out of the store toward home. She had never run so fast in her life for fear that the devil was on her heels. The older woman's words echoed in her mind, sending panic to her heart. What darkness could be lingering about her that would bring her harm, and how could this simple pouch of herbs protect her? It wasn't until she was in the security of her home that she felt safe again.

Abby glanced briefly at the pouch in her hand before putting it aside to begin preparing her evening meal. While the stew simmered, she took care of the cows and fetched water. She hummed as she worked a hopeful-sounding tune to ease the disquiet in her mind since her encounter with the older woman, Myrtle. Abby knew the woman meant no harm, but with her talk of darkness and possession…

She pressed the thoughts from her mind as she slid the bolt home, locking the bad feelings away. She prepared for bed before spooning a bowlful of supper, eager for the call of her bed. Weariness pulled at her limbs and mind with each spoonful.

So caught up in the task of eating her meager stew, Abby forgot all about the charm. Unbeknownst to her, an unseen force knocked the necklace on the floor and under the table.

In its place, unseen by Abby, a small bundle of wildflowers from the cliffs appeared.

5

Awakenings

armth. That was what Abby felt as she was dragged away from slumber and into wakefulness. Her eyes fluttered open slowly, trying to blink the sleep from her eyes. A drop of sweat traveled down her forehead, and she attempted to wipe it away from her temple.

But she couldn't move. Her limbs wouldn't respond. Her body laid pinned to the mattress as she tried to understand what was happening with her sleep-addled brain. Confusion was quickly replaced with fear.

Her breath came quick and short as she struggled against the rising panic and the invisible hold on her limbs. She glanced around the darkened bedroom. The curtain of her open window blew with the ocean breeze, but the smell of brine was so strong in her room, more potent than it usually was at night.

Abby felt a change in the atmosphere. A slight pressure pushed against her chest. As she looked around the room, a shadow emerged from a darkened corner. Her breath caught in her throat. She wanted to scream, yet nothing came out but a pathetic whimper.

A whistled tune caught her attention. It was a piece of a song she remembered fondly, and her heart began to settle in her chest. The fear was still there, but curiosity was blooming in her mind. A light touch on her cheek wiped a stray tear away that she hadn't realized had fallen.

A deep voice shushed her whimpers, and a warmth filled her chest.

"Abby."

Abby's breath caught at her name being whispered. She could almost place the voice, but the thoughts flew out of her mind.

Her blanket shifted, and Abby's eyes flicked down to the bedding. The movement was slight, but her bed linens slid slowly down her immobilized body. The chill of the ocean breeze hit what little exposed skin that was not hidden by her sleep gown, and her nipples hardened.

Her sheets hit the floor, leaving her exposed to the night air. Abby felt a soft touch on her feet and tried to shift away. It was a pulsing heat that relaxed the muscles there - a curious pressure, like a tingle when her foot fell asleep after sitting on it too long.

Abby's breath hitched when that coursing pulse slowly began to move up her legs. An ethereal caress embraced her, which electrified every nerve in her limbs. The hem of her gown rose higher and higher with each sliding touch. The deep voice shushed her again as another tear rolled down her cheek.

As frightening as the sensation was, Abby felt a fervor growing deep in her stomach. The bed jostled as a weight joined her on the mattress. The tingle continued as unseen hands trailed up her thighs, gently caressing her skin. A gasp caught in her throat at a brush against her apex, and the soft curls there were exposed as her gown continued to rise. She blushed in shame at her vulnerability.

She wanted to ask why as her clothes continued up her body until her breast heaved naked in the moonlight. Soothing caresses moved across her stomach. A spark of desire ignited as a ghostly presence carefully massaged her breasts, bringing her nipples to hardened peaks. A circle of the flesh there drew a soft moan from her, which surprised her. A sensation of fingers kneaded her, pulling more illicit sounds from her throat.

A deep moan, not her own, echoed in the tiny room, startling her. Abby held her breath as she looked around the room. The weight on her bed shifted again as the touches left her breasts and trailed down to the soft curls at her quim. As the caresses concentrated there, an intoxicating feeling shot through her body.

Abby couldn't put words to the pleasure that coursed through her. She had only felt something similar briefly as she bathed, but the intensity pulsed with such force that Abby felt like she was being warmed at her core from within. Her breath came quicker, not from fear but expectancy. Whatever was happening to her was otherworldly, and a bliss built inside her, threatening to burst forth.

Abby wanted to protest, but the words would not come. Just when she thought she couldn't feel any more bliss, an intense pleasure surged through her like a great wave, drowning her in ecstasy. Abby cried out before she felt her body relax against the mattress. She thought whatever was happening was over–until a weight rested on her.

Her name cascaded through the dark as soft intimate sounds from that deep voice. She felt a pressure at her apex, then a radiating spark of heat inside her. She shivered as her body jerked up the bed. Unseen hands caressed her arms, breasts, and hair as the pulsing movement continued. Phantom lips brushed the skin on her face, moving down her jaw to her lips. Slight pressures – tiny sparks of electrical pulses – radiated through her skin with each kiss and touch.

A now-familiar build of desire simmered under her skin, pushing her toward that cliff of ecstasy again. Deep groans mingled with her own. Her fingers tingled and twitched, catching the sheet under her. A shimmer appeared over her, with an outline forming around it. Her eyes tried to make sense of it as another wave of pleasure broke over her, and Abby cried out into the night. As she lay there panting, a groan deep and long cut through the night, and the shimmer became more focused for her eyes to see.

A face.

A man's face.

He hovered over her as a spectral hand brushed the hair from her cheek. She was overwhelmed at the vision before her. The face descended onto hers, and she felt their lips meet. An electric spark of desire made her lips prickle in a pleasurable way.

The shadow of a man pulled away as if looking at her, and she gasped. Her mind was trying to process what she saw. It wasn't possible – yet, the man before her, hovering over her, was impossible.

A stray tear fell from her eye. She wanted to reach out, but her hands still lay useless at her sides. Her lips quivered at the wave of emotion that flowed through her–shock. Joy. Amazement. Disbelief…

Longing. Those feelings pulled at her heart and mind, echoing into her soul. Abby pushed to find her voice, dreading that he would leave before she could speak his name into existence. A great groan came from her throat as she struggled, and he studied her with such concern, which turned quickly to horror. Her eyes begged him not to go as he pulled away. The shimmer faded as he left the bed and faded into the shadows.

At that moment, the hold on her broke, and she sat upright in an instant, reaching toward the spot where he had faded from view. The tears Abby had been holding broke free, and she sobbed as she stumbled out of bed. Her hands met cold stone, and she wailed with the injustice the heavens had bestowed on her. To be reunited and to have it torn away from her just as swiftly? A crueler fate, she could not imagine.

Her hands roughly grabbed her sleeping gown as she wrung it with her fingers in abject misery. Her back hit the wall, sliding down to slouch on the floor. Abby repeated one name over and over again.

"Will. Will. *Will.*"

6

Remembrances

Abby woke curled on the cold stone floor, still emotionally numb from all that had transpired. Her face felt sore from all the crying she had done after Will disappeared, groaning with stiff limbs as she stood to ready herself for the day. The sunlight that streamed in through the window seemed brighter than any day since that fateful day. Will was here, and her life was altered because of it.

Abby called out for him, but the air stayed still. She slapped her hands against the stone floor in frustration.

Why wouldn't he answer? Why would he hide from her?

"Will," she chided, "that's no way to treat me. Come out so we can talk."

Birdsong and the random moos from the cows outside seeped in through her window, but nothing more. Not a whisper, nor a touch. Just biting silence.

She shuffled around the cottage in a daze, lost in her thoughts. As she glanced toward the table, something caught her eye. Her fingers traced the petals of the small bundle of wildflowers on the table. The same flowers Will used to pick for her.

A shy smile spread on Abby's face, and she blushed as her thoughts tumbled to what had happened the night before.

What *had* happened? She had never felt such pleasure before, and it had been all Will's doing.

Will is here.

Abby could barely contain her excitement over his return. She had to tell someone, anyone. Will was back – not in the way she wanted, but alive, in a way. He had not abandoned her after all, and her prayers had been answered.

She haphazardly dressed, not caring if her hair was neat or her appearance tidy. The door slammed shut behind her as she took off down the trail to town. Her feet seemed to fly down the narrow path. She wove her way through the bustle of carts and people making their way through the streets as she maneuvered toward the docks, looking for a friendly face. She thought briefly about finding Myrtle, since the old woman had known Will, but decided against it, fearing she would be disappointed Abby hadn't worn the pouch she gave her.

The pouch.

Abby considered it strange that she hadn't seen it since yesterday evening when she made stew. The more she contemplated it, the more it puzzled her. It was as if the necklace had vanished into thin air.

Although she was preoccupied with the missing pouch, more pressing thoughts pushed her confusion away.

Abby gazed around the pier, trying to recognize faces. With no Frederick in sight, she was relieved that she didn't have to talk to him yet. As she made her way toward the warehouses, her eyes landed on a man she had not seen in a while – a man who had been good friends with Will. Abby and Will had supped many times with Edward and his lovely wife, Sarah, before the accident at sea.

But Abby didn't want to dwell on the past, and she no longer had to since William's return. She didn't know how or why, but seeing Will again was everything that she had prayed for. Dreamed of. It was as if God or whatever divine being responsible had granted her this to give her hope.

"Edward!" she called out as she ran toward him. "Mr. Finnigan!"

Edward turned his eyes toward her, and his face lit up brilliantly. "Miss Abigail Huxley!" he answered, waving for her to join him.

Abby ran up to her dear friend, panting in delight, for she had not seen him for many years. Edward looked healthy, dressed in his fine clothes, looking like the very image of prosperity. A smile bloomed on his face, and she knew that Edward had missed her as much as she missed him. He took her hand and, while bowing, placed his forehead against the back of it. His gesture was sweet and kind, one she had lacked in her life. When he righted himself, Edward smiled brightly at her.

"Sarah will be sorely disappointed that she could not join me on this trip, especially after I tell her that I got to see you."

Abby clasped her hands in front of her. "Oh, Sarah! I was going to ask how she and your babe are doing."

Edward laughed. "They are well indeed. Sarah is pregnant with our second child, which is why she could not make the journey, and Allison is a bright, precocious girl that has no fear about her."

An ache squeezed her heart. She had wanted children with Will so desperately, and here listening to Edward speak of his little one made Abby's longing for the past even stronger. And now he had another on the way? He was truly blessed.

"I am so thrilled for you both! Then why are you here instead of at home?"

"Frederick wanted to speak to me about the supply route I use to acquire the cotton for my factory. I think he wants to convince me to use him instead."

"Of course he is," Abby scoffed. "Your factory? I knew your family had a textile business, but it's yours now?"

"Aye. It is. When my father passed, I inherited the factory."

"I'm sorry to hear of his passing. You have my condolences. Is the rest of your family well?"

"Thank you. My mother is well, living with Sarah and me. My sister, Tabitha, married a fine gentleman in town recently. She is blissfully happy."

Abby was caught up in his infectious smile. She was delighted that his family was doing well in life. "So, fisherman Edward Finnigan has become a businessman? How grown-up of you!"

Someone bumped into her, and Edward reached out to steady her. The activity around them was bustling as another ship came into port.

"Here, we'd better find a quieter place to speak. One where I can watch for Frederick's arrival."

Abby nodded as she allowed herself to be led out of the fray. The noise and bustle of the activity became a buzz in the distance. She and Edward came to rest on a bench outside of the main warehouse, furthest from the docks. Abby took a deep breath while thinking of a way to bring up her situation with Will. Of all of Will's closest friends, Edward was the best person to consult about such things.

"Miss Huxley," Edward began quietly, and Abby's eyes met the concern she found there, "why didn't you let Sarah know you were engaged to Frederick?"

"Please, call me Abigail," she insisted. "You and Will were such good friends that I hoped you counted me as a friend also."

Edward nodded before meeting her eyes again. "Abigail, why are you so secretive about your engagement? One would hope you would be excited for the prospect of an agreeable match."

Abby sighed as she cast her eyes to the ground and wrung her hands in her lap. "I didn't know what to tell her. I know Frederick can provide a good life for me, but a part of me feels guilty."

Edward hummed in understanding as he sat back to lean against the wall. "Do you want to marry Frederick?"

Abby glanced at him before looking toward the docks. "At first, I thought maybe I could grow to love him. He had always been so kind and patient with me while I mourned Will. But since the engagement was announced –" Abby hesitated to speak anymore.

Edward sat forward and soothingly touched her shoulder. "Abigail, what is it?"

Abby looked into his eyes. "Please, don't say a word to Frederick," she begged.

She couldn't help the shiver that coursed through her body. Edward grasped her hands in his.

"My God, Abigail. You're trembling. What is going on?"

"Whenever I mention William, Frederick gets very angry with me," she whispered.

His body tensed, as well as his grasp on Abby's hands. "Has Frederick hurt you, Abigail? Our dear Will - God rest his soul - would never forgive me if I didn't watch out for you. Please. You can tell me."

"He has never raised a hand to me, but he has been rough and has spoken harshly to me."

Edward cursed under his breath before apologizing for saying such words in front of her. "He should not do such things to you. William was the love of your life. Your perfect match." He considered his next words carefully. "But remember, William was his best friend since childhood. Frederick has never forgiven himself for his inability to save Will that day."

Abby felt the tears pricking in her eyes when she gazed into his face. "Please tell me about that day again. What do you remember?"

Edward studied her for a moment, taken aback by her request. "You really want to hear of that terrible day?"

Abby nodded. "I've only heard about it from Frederick. I want to know what you saw."

He steeled himself before he said, "The day had been like any other fishing excursion. The skies were clear, with only a few clouds dotting the heavens. Everyone seemed to be in good spirits, for the fish were abundant. Will, Frederick, I, and a few others had been talking when the waves became rough. The Captain called for us to secure the gear and baskets. Frederick was with Timson and me, taking the rope and looping through the baskets as William, Archie, Billy, and Michael worked on securing the fishing gear and nets.

When the water started crashing over the rail, the deck became slippery from some fish guts we used as bait. The boat rocked as everyone attempted to moor themselves to the ship. That's when the first massive wave battered onto the deck. Billy was swept overboard, and we lost track of him quickly in the storm.

There was shouting over the roar of the storm. Then the next wave hit. And as the water receded, Archie's line broke, dragging Archie from the deck. Will grabbed the boy as he went over the railing. The ship lurched suddenly, sending Will over the rail with Archie. Even though he was still roped to the deck, Will had, fortunately, grabbed the railing with his hand.

Frederick untied himself and raced to Will's aid, ignoring the shouts of myself and others. Frederick tried grabbing Will's arm to pull him up, but Will must have been too heavy, or wrapped up in the rope. They exchanged some words as Frederick kept trying to heave Will onboard.

Suddenly, the rope must have snapped because it came flying back as Frederick fell backward onto the deck. He scrambled to his feet and ran to the rail, but Will was gone. Frederick screamed for him as we watched helplessly.

I yelled for him to tie himself down, and slowly, almost numbly, he secured himself with the rope Will had left behind." Edward cleared his throat and blinked away his tears before glancing at Abby. "Oh, Abigail. I told you it would be too much for you to hear. Now I have made you cry."

Abby wiped tears from her cheeks before dabbing her nose with her shawl. "No. No. I needed to hear it. Did you try to search the area after the storm?"

Edward grimly nodded. "We did. We found some baskets that had broken loose, but no bodies."

No Will.

Abby shifted in her seat. "I appreciate your candor. Frederick never went into the details of what happened. Just that it did, and I was so broken at the time, the details didn't matter."

"I'm sure."

Abby felt a sudden urgency to tell him about seeing Will the previous night. She wasn't sure how he would handle the news or if he would dismiss her. A nervousness coursed through her veins, causing her to spring to her feet and pace before him.

"Dearest Mr. Finnigan, I have something to tell you."

"It sounds very serious."

Abby groaned before she sat next to him again. "It is. Promise you won't laugh or think I'm deranged?"

Edward laughed uncomfortably before he set his face serious when she gave him a scathing glance. "I promise."

Abby faltered a moment, then took a steadying breath. "I think William is visiting me."

Edward's mouth turned down as he absorbed her words. "But William is dead."

"Yes," she insisted. "His ghost has been visiting me."

Edward mumbled a few unsavory words under his breath. "And what makes you think this is Will?"

"Well, it looks and talks like him. You see, he is unhappy about my engagement to Frederick–"

He held up his hand, cutting her off. "The only one unhappy about this engagement seems to be you, Abigail."

"Well, yes, but not all betrothals are about love, Mr. Finnigan."

"Maybe these dreams of Will are a manifestation of your fears or unhappiness."

"Well, maybe, but perhaps it *is* Will."

Edward sighed as he took her hands. "If you don't want this marriage, break it off cleanly."

She bit her bottom lip as she thought. She wished she could break the engagement, but the money was the issue. "I can't. Father already spent the bride's price. There is no way he would be able to return it to Frederick. Nor can I afford to do it. The money Will left me is near its end."

He growled in frustration. "No. I will not allow you to enter a marriage that would cause you sadness. You have been through enough sorrow. I should never have left. If I had stayed, you wouldn't have been in this mess."

"You had a duty to your family. There was no way you could have foreseen this."

"No. That is wrong. I knew Frederick would eventually ask for your hand."

"Wh-what?"

"When Will proclaimed he would woo you to wife, Frederick became angry. Oh, he didn't show Will his anger. I found him punching a sawdust bag hanging in one of the warehouses. He was furious that Will thought he had some claim on you."

Abby hung on every word. Edward was confirming this defect she hadn't known to dwell in Frederick until recently: the cruel face he hid from her for so long.

"Well, he has a claim on me now."

Sorrow washed over her. She had run out of choices. Abby refused to be a burden to her friends and family. She knew what she had to do even though it was problematic and undesirable. She hoped that one day, maybe some kind of happiness would come from this union.

"Look, Abigail, I could give you the money you need to break the engagement–"

"Who's breaking the engagement?" Frederick snapped as he stepped up to them.

Both of them were startled at the sound of his angry voice.

"Sebastian's second daughter," Abby quickly interjected.

Edward threw her a sharp look as he pressed his lips together.

Frederick's face relaxed. "Oh, I'm sorry to hear that. He must be disappointed. I'm sure he had found a fine match for her."

Abby nodded. "Yes, but Emilia was unhappy with the man's sour mood. Sebastian is such a romantic that he gave in to her request. Now he must repay her suitor, but his finances have been stretched with the expansion of his firm. Mr. Finnigan was kindly offering to assist since he's been so close to my family."

Frederick nodded toward Edward. "I'm sure Sebastian has everything well in hand financially. No need to assume the worst, otherwise, he would have not allowed the breaking of the engagement. I am sure they will find a better match for her. Not everyone can be like you and me, my love."

She felt herself pale as she glanced at Edward. "Yes, we are very fortunate."

Edward's eyes pleaded with her, but Abby stood and turned to Frederick. "Well, Mr. Finnigan has told me he is here to discuss business with you, so if you will excuse me, I will let you do it."

Frederick smiled approvingly at her before kissing her forehead. "Wonderful. Will I see you later?"

"I was going to shop for supplies before heading back home. I am still trying to prepare my wedding gown. Lots of embroidery to do."

Frederick seemed to approve of her answer, leaving her an opportunity to escape.

"Mr. Finnigan, please tell Sarah I miss her terribly and wish I could hug your little one. And congratulations again on your little one to come."

Edward's eyes pleaded for her to stay. She could see that he wanted to take away her burden, but she knew what needed to be done. There was no turning back. What broke Abby's heart was that Edward didn't believe her about Will. He dismissed Will like he was a dream.

Abby hurried down the street and stopped in several stores to procure food and other necessary items for the next few days.

She was going to attempt to communicate with Will and find out why he had returned.

She had to find out. Her heart couldn't rest until things between them were set right.

She was in such a hurry, she barely saw Myrtle sweeping the front porch of her shop. The old woman called out to her, and Abby turned toward the porch. As Abby approached, Myrtle's face contorted into a strange expression of horror.

Myrtle grabbed her arm. "Please tell me, child, that you are wearing the charm."

"The necklace?"

"Yes. Show it to me."

Abby pulled away from Myrtle, wrapping her shawl tighter around her shoulders. *Why was the necklace so important?* "I must have forgotten it at home."

Myrtle gasped. "You never wore it, did you? Miss Abigail, I cannot stress the importance that you need to wear it."

"I don't understand why it's so important! It's just some pouch of herbs." Abby scoffed.

Myrtle studied her for a moment. "Something has happened."

Abby blushed as she thought back to last evening. "I don't know what you mean."

The denial leapt from her lips, hoping that the older woman would not question any further.

"Miss Abigail, have your dreams returned? Or is it something more?" Her eyes narrowed as they roamed Abby's figure; as if looking for something out of place. "Your aura has dimmed, and there's a strangeness to it. Like–" Myrtle pursed her lips in thought.

Abby wanted to flee from her knowing eyes. "I appreciate your concern, Myrtle, but–"

Myrtle's intense stare stole the words from Abby's mouth. "You must not let it happen again. You are playing with fire, dear child, if you think you can handle this on your own. The spirit world does not belong with our world. Dire consequences happen when the two collide."

"I still don't know what you are talking about."

"Just because you believe something doesn't make it true." Myrtle took Abby's hands in hers. "Please, Miss Abigail, for the sake of your life and soul, wear the charm," Myrtle begged.

Abby's heart raced as she looked into the older woman's eyes. *My life? My soul?* What was she talking about? It was only Will, and Will would never hurt her.

"No," Abby murmured. "You can't take him."

She pulled away from Myrtle and rushed toward the cliffs. No one was ever going to take him from her again.

7

Bonded

Abby couldn't remember how many days had passed. Her naked body glistened in the moonlight shining through her window as she reclined across the bed. She enjoyed the feel of the cool night air while she stood to get a drink from the water bucket. She could feel the hungry gaze of Will as she moved through the room, her long, flowing auburn hair stirring as she walked.

When she had returned from town, Will's presence had been there waiting for her. Maybe he could sense her need for him, or perhaps he knew her mind better than she did, for all thoughts or concerns of anything else in Abby's life disappeared at the first brush of his hand against her. She gave herself willingly to his whim, drowning herself in pleasure.

Abby glanced back to the bed. Will's outline and features were more apparent than they had been before. She could see the glint in his eyes and the soft curve of his mouth in the candlelight as he pressed his lips together and released. No longer was she frozen when he came to her wantonly. She could almost touch his hair, its faint presence just a wisp of awareness.

His body and hands roamed her body freely, bringing her waves of pleasure upon pleasure. She could feel the exhaustion from their activities throughout her body.

"Abby," Will called to her softly, "come back to bed."

Abby felt that now-familiar warmth already building in her body at the mere sound of his deep voice. Even though she had barely slept or eaten, she didn't care anymore. She saw a slight movement, and Will was behind her in the blink of an eye, embracing her. Enveloping her in such love she thought she had lost.

Will was more like an energy that moved around her and through her, pulsating with comfort and bliss. Abby didn't know that sex, or what she guessed was a form of sex, could feel like that.

"Come back to bed," he growled in her ear.

Abby groaned as she smiled. "I can't do it anymore, Will. I'm so tired."

"Please," he begged. "I need to feel your pleasure again."

Abby drank a full cup of water before slamming the wooden cup onto the table. The same table was now littered with wildflowers from Will, bringing a sweet smell to the little cottage. Abby's stomach growled in protest, so she grabbed a piece of cheese from a basket that sat amongst the flowers. She nibbled on it as she made her way to the bed.

Will's essence flew across the room, circling the bed as she sat upon it. He let her finish her small snack, and watched her intently as she lay down—then, he was on her again. Her body convulsed with ecstasy as his mouth and hands wandered her body. Each time, she could almost feel the calluses of his fingers. The softness of his hair on her skin. The weight of his body on hers.

The sounds of their pleasure echoed off the walls of the cottage. This dwelling was no longer just hers anymore. Will had built and given this house to her to keep her safe. It eyes now their haven between two worlds.

More than that, Will had claimed her body, inside and out. Her maidenhead might still be intact, but that didn't matter anymore. In her mind, Frederick no longer had a privilege to her body either. She was Will's–and *only* Will's.

Abby cried out as Will pulled a burst of passion from her body. Her wet release joined the mess of her arousal on her sheets. She panted as she reached out to caress his face. His handsome features were so distinct now that touching him seemed possible. When her fingers passed through his cheek, she wanted to cry.

A tear streaked down her face, and Will cooed, "Now, now, my dearest love. Have no fear. It will be soon."

A wave of exhaustion tried to drown her in sleep. Abby struggled to keep her eyes open.

"Will, I am so tired."

Her voice was faint and distant in her own ears. Will kissed her cheek.

"Sleep, my love. I will continue to watch over you as you rest."

She hummed as she closed her eyes, but Will did not leave her. Even in dreams, Will's loving embrace persisted like he was afraid of losing time.

Warm lips on her breast.

A calloused hand on her hip.

A knock at the door.

Abby's eyebrows furrowed in confusion as she slowly roused from her slumber. Who was knocking on the door? Her eyes fluttered open to stare into Will's face, whose body had stilled. A deep growl came from his chest as his mouth dipped down into a frown.

"Miss Abigail!" a voice called through the door before another knock followed.

Abby sighed. "It's Myrtle Ravenwood," she whined. "If I don't see her, she won't go away."

Will's eyebrows rose in surprise. "Myrtle Ravenwood? What is she doing here in the middle of the night?"

Abby scoffed as a heavy pounding sounded on her door. "I don't know what she wants if I don't answer the door."

Will made a frustrated sound. "Fine. But get rid of her soon."

He tried to kiss her lips, but Abby only felt a ghost of pressure, leaving her wanting more. Will withdrew from the bed and seemed to have trouble fading. Abby attempted to stand, but her legs collapsed under her. She didn't realize how weak she had become from lack of sleep and food.

The knock came again, and Abby called that she was coming. She pulled herself upright and slipped her sleeping gown over her head. Abby dressed while leaning against the bed, feeling Will's eyes still watching her. As she made her way across the room, she used the walls and furniture to keep herself from falling.

Exhausted, she threw the bolt free and pulled the door open. Myrtle's expression turned from relief to concern as she reached forward to help as Abby crumpled to the floor.

"My God, child, what have you done to yourself?" Myrtle huffed. "No, on second thought, don't tell me what you have been doing. I have an idea of what you have endured." She helped Abby out of the doorway so she could shut the door before taking her to the closest chair.

Abby whispered her thanks as Myrtle fussed over her unkempt hair and filthy clothes. Myrtle ran a brush through Abby's hair while mumbling to herself.

"Young people… thinking with other parts of their bodies than their brains."

Myrtle cursed at a particularly nasty knot as she worked the plaits in Abby's hair. Abby could barely concentrate and struggled to keep her eyes open.

"Myrtle, why are you here?"

A tidy red braid plopped onto Abby's shoulder as Myrtle released her hair. The old woman leaned down to pick up a basket and place it on the table, tsking at the litter of flowers.

"A sentimentalist as always, that boy," she mumbled, pulling out a bottle of milk. Then came a meat pie that smelled divine, and a large chunk of cheese wrapped in cloth.

Abby groaned as she dug her fingers into the meat pie and ate it fervently. Myrtle made a noise of disapproval before sitting in a chair next to her.

"Thought you would need food because it has been three days since we last spoke. And because I knew you wouldn't listen to me. I knew that boy would keep you" –Myrtle paused as she thought of perfect words–"let's just say, *preoccupied.*"

Abby snorted, unladylike, into a handful of pie. "That's an understatement." She stilled as she studied the older woman for a moment. "You know Will's here."

Myrtle nodded slowly as Abby took another bite of pie. "He's a little hard to miss, hovering around you like he is." She gazed over Abby's shoulder. "William, you need to give the woman a moment to breathe and eat," she scolded, and Will's comforting warmth pulled away obediently.

Abby gazed upon the woman before her with new eyes.

"How?"

"How can I see him?" Myrtle replied, and Abby nodded. "It is a gift of sight that I have always thought I would be better off without. But it is useful from time to time, like now."

Abby licked her fingers clean before she worked the cork in the milk bottle between her thumbs until it popped out. The milk went heavenly down her throat. She blushed at the realization of how much Myrtle knew.

"If you don't rest and eat, he will kill you," Myrtle huffed.

Shocked, Abby set down her drink. This woman knew Will - was fond of him. *How can she ever think...?* "No, Will would never hurt me."

"Not intentionally, he wouldn't. But your aura is so dim, Miss Abigail. Will is draining your energy too fast. Another day of this and he would have killed you, which would have been no bother to him since you would both be together in the afterlife."

Abby stared at her with a mouthful of cheese. She slowly chewed as she thought through what Myrtle had said. Her weakness in her limbs. Her lightheadedness. Her tiredness. When Abby strung the pieces together, Myrtle's reasoning made sense.

Myrtle smiled as she saw Abby's resigned look. "You know I speak the truth."

She produced a pouch from under the table – the same sack Myrtle had given her only days before.

That is where it went.

"You need to wear this. William has latched onto your soul and life force. You are now bonded in this life and beyond. My job is to keep you in this one. Wear this charm, and it gives us another day to figure out what we need to do."

Abby took the necklace from the older woman's hand. It felt

heavier than it had before. The thought baffled her. As she contemplated Myrtle's words, she asked, "How do you know William? Pardon me for asking, but you seem very familiar with him."

Myrtle sighed as she sat back in her chair. Weariness drew the lines of her mouth down as she steadied her thoughts. The weight of her unspoken words struck Abby speechless while the older woman smoothed her woolen skirt.

Myrtle's knowing eyes softened. "I knew William when he was a child in Whitby. He, at the time, lived with his mother and father. His father was a fisherman, just like William, and his mother was a fine lady from a noble background. How she ended up with a lowly fisherman was anyone's guess, but they were delightfully content in their choice.

Time passed, and William grew into a young lad of ten when his first bout of bad luck happened. His mother had fallen ill, and I was called in by his father to help her. At the time, I had a shop in Whitby and was well-known for my healing potions. In addition, I was a good friend of his mother's. Unfortunately, I was unable to save her.

From time to time, after she was gone, I would check in on William and his father. By the time William was sixteen, he had joined the same fishing crew as his father. Then, the second stroke of fated misfortune hit William; his father suffered a heart attack and passed.

I encouraged William to take his meager inheritance and begin a new life. So, he packed what was left of his household and moved here, where he met you, the love of his life. William wrote to me about you since I was the closest thing to family he had left."

Abby sniffled as tears fell down her face. "My poor William.

He had lost so much."

Abby forgot her food in her sorrow. William had wanted a big family because he had none left of his own. How Abby would have gladly given it to him. A comforting, unseen hand brushed her shoulders.

"I know," Will whispered into her ear.

Myrtle clapped her hands. "Enough sadness. Let's get you cleaned up and to bed with that charm around your neck."

Abby felt a tug on the leather strap, almost pulling the necklace from her hands. Will was unhappy about the matter.

"William will be upset, won't he?"

Myrtle chuckled. "Aye, he will be. But you need your rest to recover from his amorous endeavors, I suspect."

Abby felt her blush deepen at Myrtle's words. Myrtle poured water into a washing bowl and handed Abby a cloth to clean herself.

"I will strip the bed linens and put fresh ones on while you bathe."

They both worked quietly until each had finished their tasks. Abby dressed in a clean sleeping gown as Myrtle tucked the last of the sheets on the bed. Myrtle turned to eye the charm in Abby's hand.

"Now, don the charm, young lady. It would be best if you had your rest and strength. Besides, that boy has given you quite a load of wash to do."

A spectral hand touched her cheek as if reminding her of his affection. The charm almost fell from her hand, and she closed a fist around it. Will was trying to get rid of the amulet.

Abby took the leather cord and draped it around her neck. The atmosphere of the cottage changed, becoming lighter, like a heavy weight had been lifted. Will's touch disappeared. An immense peace wrapped around Abby, and the fatigue caught up with her.

Myrtle gave her a motherly smile as she patted her shoulder. "Good girl. Now, don't take it off until you are recovered."

Abby yawned widely as she tried to cover her mouth. "How long will that take?"

"Several days. Rest. Eat. There is enough food in the basket to get you through the next few days. Come see me when you are recovered. We have lots to discuss."

"Thank you, Myrtle."

Myrtle nodded as she made her way to the door. "Bolt the door tight, child. And sleep well."

Abby followed Myrtle to the door and bade her farewell before bolting the door like she had been directed. The older woman was right; she needed to take care of herself.

Will was everything she wanted. He has filled her life with such joy and passion, but if she wanted to continue to be with him, her health and well-being must come first.

As she tucked herself in her blankets, a deep groan surrounded her. Things in the cottage began banging and moving as if in anger for a long moment –until all became quiet again. Abby sat up to glance around the room. She never realized how eerie the silence was since Will returned to her.

"Will?" she called, but there was no answer. Abby realized for the first time in her life she had never felt so alone.

8

Decisions & Consequences

The next few days passed in near silence. The cottage was quiet with an air about it like it was waiting for something to happen. Abby kept herself busy with chores and taking care of herself. She had no urge to go to town or see anyone because the one person she wanted to see the most was out of her reach while she wore the charm.

In that time, Will didn't try to contact or touch her. Sadness sank into her very being, dragging her down with misery. The ache she felt for him almost made her remove the necklace and embrace him again.

Sleep didn't come easily for her, either. Abby was restless every night after that first night of dreamless sleep. Though she felt less drained than the night Myrtle came to call, she wondered if all the loneliness was worth the separation.

But the severance of their bond did the trick, and Abby began to feel more like herself. The weariness faded, but, in the end, she grew restless. That was the morning she woke late, and the sun had climbed high in the sky. It felt like any other day, but Abby knew differently. She remembered it was the tenth anniversary of Will's death. A day that changed her life forever.

Taking the last of the jam, bread, and cheese from the basket, she partook of a measly breakfast, knowing that she would have to venture into town and face Myrtle again. Not that she dreaded seeing the older woman. She had developed quite a fondness for the older woman, but a decision loomed over Abby. One that needed to be answered: what to do about Will?

She set about readying herself for the day. Fetching fresh water to drink and wash her face. Dressing and donning her shoes. As she closed the door with Myrtle's basket in hand, Abby made her way down the narrow cliff path to town. The afternoon sunlight shined harsh on her eyes, making them water.

Once Abby got into town, she headed in the direction of Myrtle's shop. She found herself whistling as she walked, which was strange, as it was not her habit. The tune was a memory of something she had heard a long time ago. Abby watched as the basket swung in her hand, ignoring all around her.

"Abigail!"

The sound of her name snapped her out of her reverie. Abby stopped walking and glanced around to find Frederick crossing the street toward her.

"Abigail. There you are. I haven't seen you in a few days." Frederick's eyes studied her face. "Abigail, are you well?"

His hand came to touch her cheek. Abby wanted to pull away from him, but when she saw the deep concern in his eyes, she stood her ground.

"I am better, thank you," she said softly.

Frederick admonished himself. "When you didn't come into town yesterday, I should have checked on you, but several shipments came in from the train at Whitby, and the boats–"

Frederick growled in frustration. "What kind of man doesn't check on his fiancée? One that doesn't deserve her."

His face fell, and Abby's stomach clenched at his words. It felt like an act to her, this feigning devotion. Lies to draw her in as he solidified his insistence on marriage, on controlling her, on possessing her. He had fooled her brother, Sebastian into supporting the match and championing the proposal. If she was going to escape Frederick's deceit, she needed to play along.

She reached out to take his hand, caressing it.

"Myrtle came to check on me a few days ago and brought me some medicine and food. She took care of me for a moment and ensured I was comfortable."

"You truly have been in my waking thoughts, hoping that you would appear, but work –"

"Frederick, I already absolved you of your guilt. I am faring better and thinking clearer than I have in a long time." His eyes found hers, and Abby tried to give him her best smile. With the return of Will, she didn't want Frederick to suspect her true intentions. "All these years, you have watched over me and made sure that I was well. You can't help that you're a successful businessman. You must expect to be pulled in many directions at one time."

"That's not an excuse, Abigail. You are going to be my wife soon. I should make time for you always, because I care for you. Ardently."

He took their clasped hands and brought hers to his lips, kissing them gently. Abby cringed at the brush of his lips against her skin. Every touch reminded her of how wrong this engagement was. But what other choice did she have? She was trapped, forced by circumstance into a marriage with a man she didn't want.

She thought of Will. The man she knew was gone, lost to the sea. The ghost in her cottage was just the echo of the man, one that she couldn't touch. Any real future with Will was gone. There would be no children. No growing old together.

But here, with this man in front of her, she had that opportunity. True, she didn't love him; at least, not like she loved Will. But Abby could have a future with Frederick. Yet his behavior since the engagement… Abby shuddered as she remembered his anger and envy toward her, and his disregard for her memory of Will.

But now that Will had returned, maybe Abby had another option. A choice that frightened her… but it was better than the alternative.

"I know you care for me," she breathed, playing along

"Let me take care of you this evening. I will buy you an early supper at the inn. We'll talk, and I'll walk you home to assure that you are settled and comfortable."

Abby gazed into his hopeful eyes. Maybe Edward had talked to him about his behavior. Perhaps Frederick was trying to make amends with her for these past few months. No matter the reason, Abby found herself cautious regarding his attention to her.

"I would be pleased to join you," she said guardedly.

The boyish grin she received gave her a sense of hope. "Wonderful." Frederick glanced behind him at the sound of a shout from the docks, beckoning him. "I have a few things to settle, and then I will be finished for the day. Meet me at the inn? Say, in a half-hour?"

"I will. I just need to look in at Myrtle's shop to return her basket and give my thanks."

Frederick nodded as he kissed her hand once more before backing away. "I will see you soon, my love."

His declaration of affection set Abby aback. She felt the blood drain from her face. Abby forced herself to smile at him before he hurried off. As Frederick's presence disappeared, Abby's smile fell to a frown. What was she doing? She gazed at the offending hand that Frederick had kissed. She didn't have time for second-guessing herself or falling for Frederick's charms again.

Abby hurried down the street to the shop. The bell barely sounded before Abby closed the door quickly behind her. She swiftly bypassed the shelves and tables, heading straight for the counter.

"Myrtle!" Abby called as she placed the basket on the counter.

"Back here," Myrtle answered, her voice muffled by a curtain across a doorway that led to the backroom.

Abby made her way through the curtain. Several lanterns lit the backroom, and boxes were stacked against the wall. A table was littered with flowers, herbal plants, and other whatnots, along with bowls, mortar, pestle, and bottles. Myrtle sat behind the table, working her gnarled fingers to strip leaves from a thin branch.

"Come. Sit. Sit, child."

Myrtle nodded toward the seat opposite her. Abby made her way to the cushioned chair as her fingers fumbled with the pouch hanging from the charm around her neck.

The old woman glanced up to smile at her, but something stopped her from completing the task. Myrtle immediately stood and came to take Abby's hands.

"Miss Abigail, are you well?"

Abby looked down at their clasped hands, then back up into

Myrtle's eyes. "Yes, I am better."

Myrtle studied her. "You are awfully pale. Are you sleeping better?"

"The first night, I fell straight asleep."

Myrtle waited for her to say more. "And the other nights?"

Abby groaned. "I could barely sleep. I was so restless and couldn't get comfortable."

Myrtle squinted at her before pulling away to pace the room. She mumbled to herself, and Abby caught a phrase here and there.

"-charm should have worked-"

"-spirits affected-"

"-must have miscalculated-"

Abby watched Myrtle's small feet carry her back and forth across the tiny room before Myrtle suddenly turned back to her.

"And you wore the charm the entire time, even while bathing and sleeping?"

Abby blinked. "Why yes, just like you told me. You said never to take it off."

Myrtle threw her hands in the air and made a loud huff of frustration as she made her way back to her chair.

"The charm should be keeping William's spirit away."

"It is, and I know he is unhappy with it. He has left me alone. But I am melancholic, too. I eat, but food has no taste. I try to sleep, but I get no rest, nor do I dream. I feel like I am walking in a daze, not really alive."

Myrtle hummed, her fingers fumbling with a flower's petals. "That is the side effect of the bond. I got to you too late." She sat back to contemplate before she leaned forward to take Abby's hand. "I will be frank with you. If you want William to return to the afterlife, we can perform a ritual that will break the bond and free you to live without his interference. But if you want William to stay and remove that necklace, William will absorb your energy until you join him in the afterlife. I know he doesn't mean to harm you, but it is the nature of spirits. They want to feel and taste what it is to be alive again."

"Will coming back was an answer to my prayers," Abby whispered. "After he disappeared, I prayed to God. To every deity. Fae. The spirits of the ocean. I begged. Bargained. Pleaded. And I waited. For ten long years, I waited for a sign." She wiped a tear as it fell down her cheek.

"And you got your answer, didn't you?"

"Yes, he was dead, Myrtle. And along with it, everything I wanted in life. He was my life, Myrtle." Her tears flowed down her face, and her hands angrily wiped what she could from her cheeks. She took a deep breath and let out a shaky exhale. "Myrtle, I can't live without him. I don't want to live in a world where Will is not."

Myrtle gave her a severe look. "Child, you don't know what that means. You're-"

"Young, I know. But everything I ever wanted was with Will. My hopes. My dreams. A family. I truly don't wish that with anyone else. And if that means I give in and let Will take me, then so be it." Abby stood swiftly, taking the necklace off to place it on the table before Myrtle.

Myrtle gazed up at her in shock. "Miss Abigail-"

Abby cut off any words of protest. She couldn't help but look upon Myrtle with great fondness. "No. I appreciate all the concern and care you have given me, but my mind is made up. I have contemplated my fate these past few days, and I choose Will. It's better than this hell I have lived in since he was taken from me."

Suddenly, the curtain was shoved to the side, and Abby turned to see the pale face of Frederick gazing at her in horror.

"Abigail," he rasped as his voice broke with raw emotion.

She couldn't deal with him, or with anything else. So, she ran.

9

Surrender

Abby's feet took her through the town like she was flying. She heard the call of her name from different people, but she wanted nothing to do with them. Even the wind seemed to take her faster to the arms of her lover as she ran up the cliff pass. Her heart beat fast, but it had nothing to do with her sprint. Her breath was steady, filling her with confidence, for she knew who awaited her at the top of the cliff.

She threw the door open only to find the cottage empty. Abby glanced around the small room, hoping for a glimpse of Will. But there was nothing. Not a sound. Not a blur of motion. Abby turned to close the door, throwing the bolt in place.

At that moment, the air surrounding her changed, and Will pressed himself against her back. Her skin tingled as he touched her body. Abby turned to see his handsome face peering down at her. He stroked where the charm pouch had rested on her chest.

"You came back," Will whispered with a voice that echoed slightly.

Abby nodded. "I made my choice."

His eyes flicked up to hers. "And?"

Abby giggled as she moved away from him. She sat down to unlace her boots. "Isn't it obvious, Will?"

She felt Will's touch on her head, closing her eyes to enjoy the tingle of pleasure. Abby understood that she was giving a bit of herself to him with every touch. Her second boot joined its mate under the table. She draped her shawl over the back of the chair as she stood to meet Will again.

Will studied her face as he caressed her body, and a sigh escaped her lips. "You chose me."

Abby could hear the relief in his voice. It was a resolve that she felt deep within her. She had chosen him and had no regrets.

"I heard what Myrtle told you. Being with me could cause your death," he remarked mournfully. He withdrew from her. "I don't want to hurt you, Abby."

Abby tried to touch his face. "You could never hurt me, my love."

He moved about the room, and she waited, as she could feel Will's emotions rolling through her.

"I want to touch you, Will. Please let me touch you," she begged.

His words whispered in her ear. "Soon."

His touch lingered as it moved down her arms and pressed against her back. Her body responded as all her nerves lit on fire, as her arousal ignited, pulsing through her veins. She gasped at the suddenness of the bliss roaring through her. He hummed his pleasure, his voice rough as he groaned.

"Please," she begged as he wrapped his spectral arms around her again, hands moving up her chest.

"Let me feel your pleasure, Abby," he growled in her ear. "Only I can give you such bliss. Me, and no other."

One phantom hand stayed at her stomach while the other rested at her neck gently until his touches explored every inch of her. Abby gasped at the whirlwind of his divine caresses. She could feel her soul singing in time with Will's.

The door rattled in its frame, and Will withdrew. Abby's heart raced as she stared at the door, her knees weak. Whoever stood behind the door pounded loudly, and Abby squeaked in fear.

"Abigail! Open the door!" a voice called.

"Frederick," Abby gasped as she turned to find Will for comfort, but he was gone.

Frederick's fist made contact with the oak door. "Abigail, please! I implore you! Open the door!"

She had no choice but to let him in. Despite her devotion to Will, denying her betrothed entrance to her home defied all the laws of society. He would force his entrance one way or another, and she would pay the price for her noncompliance. Abby trembled as she reached for the bolt and threw it open. She barely moved away from the door when Frederick roughly pushed inside. Abby tried to steady her beating heart as Frederick glanced around the room. His eyes were wild with jealousy.

"Who was with you in here?"

"No one," Abby retorted.

"I heard him." Frederick stomped about the room, looking in every corner. "Who dares touch what is mine?"

Abby stood aghast at his words. "I am not yours yet," she hissed.

Frederick rounded on her and pointed a finger. "You are my betrothed!"

"And yet, I am not your wife."

Abby watched as Frederick seethed in front of her, hands clenching and unclenching into fists. He studied her as she stood in front of him.

"I heard it all," he snarled. "I came to fetch you from Myrtle's because I had finished my duties for the day and heard whispers in the back room when no one greeted me at the front of the shop." He prowled closer to her as he stared at her intently. "How can you choose a man that is dead–over *me*? Are you so miserable in this world that you would rather perish than live a life with me?"

"I chose happiness over what I have felt these past ten years."

"Happiness?" Frederick scoffed. "How can you ever be happy with only a memory of a man long gone, his body long-decayed at the bottom of the ocean?"

Abby felt herself stand straighter. "He is not long gone. He is with me even now."

Frederick burst out into laughter that frightened Abby with its ferocity. "You are delusional. Edward tried to buy off your betrothal to me, stating that you were not ready for marriage."

He was so close to her that she could smell the faint hint of tobacco on his shirt. His glare burned into her skin as his eyes searched her face. "You lied to me, Abigail. Straight to my face, humiliating me in front of Edward." He grabbed her jaw, dragging her closer. "There was no broken engagement for Sebastian's daughter, was there?"

"No."

He grunted as he roughly released her. Abby stumbled away from him as disgust churned her insides. She needed to leave, run, but he stood in her way. "I say you wish not to move forward because you are trapped in the past."

A wave of deep anger grew inside Abby–something she

recognized as a feeling coming from her lost love–and a fury welled up that matched her own. William wasn't her past. He was her future, and nothing Frederick could say would change that.

"I do not look to the past, Frederick. My future is with Will here. And you are not part of it."

"William is not here. He is gone." A look of pity softened his face as his knuckle caressed her cheek before pulling away from her.

Nausea coursed through her as she recoiled from his touch. She didn't want his pity, nor his affection. "You should not be here. I must ask you to leave."

A smug smile spread on his face. "After our discussion earlier, I decided I couldn't let you be on your own with no one to care for you. The thought of you being all alone up here, ill, did not sit well with me. So I have spoken to the Vicar, and we are to wed immediately."

"What? You can't do that!"

"I can, and I will. After I spoke to the Vicar this morning, I sent word to your brother in London. I was going to tell you at lunch today, but I am telling you now since you ran from me. Tomorrow, you will be my bride, and then we can be rid of this house and the memory of William Johnson for good."

A sob caught in Abby's throat as Frederick gave her one final glance before storming out of the cottage and slamming the door behind him. Under the weight of the situation, Abby collapsed onto the floor, weeping.

Storm clouds darkened the sky as the sun rushed to set onto the ocean's dark horizon while Abby tried to control the tears falling from her eyes. If she wanted to flee Frederick's grasp, she must leave, but where should she go? Sebastian and Penelope were in London, while Edward and Sarah were in Manchester. Abby looked around her home. But how could she leave Will?

A wail of abject misery came from her chest as she sat there on the cold, stone floor crying her pain and anger. As she inhaled deeply, she caught the scent of lavender and musk – a smell she hadn't breathed in for years. Something brushed the tears from her face and gently touched her hair.

"There now, my love," she heard Will's deep voice whisper tenderly to her. "All will be well. You will not marry Frederick."

Abby sniffled as she tried to catch her breath. She opened her eyes to find brown ones gazing lovingly at her. To her surprise, Will kneeled before her. Pale features and blonde hair bloomed into being before her eyes, just like they had looked those ten years before. His plush lips pushed into a thin line before releasing as he watched her curious glances.

Abby reached out with shaking fingers to brush the tips against his cheek–and this time, they made contact. His skin was warm, and she could feel the stubble on his jaw just at the surface. Her eyes shot up to meet his as her hand moved into his soft, blonde hair.

"Will?" she barely whispered.

He barked a laugh as his hand cupped her face, his thumb brushing along her lips. "Abby, my love."

She could see the tears forming in his eyes, and placed her hand on his chest. His heart thumped happily in his torso under her touch.

He is alive.

And on the day of the tenth anniversary of his death, William Johnson greeted the love of his life with a searing kiss.

10

Ardor & Seduction

Will's lips were warm and soft, just as she remembered them. His hands and arms caged her in, and he pulled her close. When their kiss finally broke, Abby gasped for air.

"I thought I would never be able to do that again," Will said as he rested his forehead on hers.

Abby gazed into his eyes. "What sort of magic is this? Is this even real?" She cupped his face. "I can touch you and taste you." Tears fell down her cheek as joy overflowed in her heart. "If this is a dream, I never wish to awaken."

"Oh, my love. In a way, I wish it was so. But this is real. I live and breathe at this moment because of you."

Abby's brows furrowed at his words. "What do you mean?"

Will sat on the floor, his arm resting on his upright, bent knee. "It's complicated."

"Complicated." Her look of disdain told of her lack of amusement at his answer. "That's all you can say about this miracle? Just complicated?"

Will rolled his eyes at her before standing to walk to the

table. "Please tell me you have food." He rummaged through the basket there before moving to the cabinets beside the stove.

"You are really going to ignore me?" Abby scoffed as she stood to join him. Will was dressed as he had been on that fateful day - shirt, pants with suspenders, and boots - minus his pea coat and knit cap. Edward had told her those things had been lost in the storm along with Will.

"I'm hungry," he said matter-of-factly as he grabbed a piece of cheese. He popped it in his mouth, closing his eyes in pleasure.

Abby stood there watching him with her arms crossed over her chest. He offered her a piece of cheese, but she ignored him, so he ate it.

"Will."

His eyes flicked up to meet hers. "Abby."

Abby groaned in frustration and stomped off to sit on the bed. A glimmer sparked in Will's eyes as he watched her. He rubbed his hands together to rid them of any crumbs.

"What day is it? More specifically, what makes this day unique?"

Abby thought for a moment. "It's the anniversary of your death."

A grin blossomed on his face. "Exactly."

"What does it matter anymore? You're alive now."

Will cringed, and Abby's heart dropped into her stomach. He rubbed his fingers across his mouth but did not answer her.

"Will, you are alive. You breathe. Your heart beats. You. Are. Alive." Abby felt the need to stress that what she saw with her own eyes was real and tangible and genuine.

He came to stand before her. "Yes, all of that is true."

Will's hand stroked her hair before he took the hairpin out. Her hair cascaded down her back, and Will's eyes delighted at the sight of it. His fingers brushed through her locks as he watched their journey.

"I've always wanted to do that, too."

Abby watched him carefully as he was lost in thought. "Will," she chided. "You're not making any sense. None of this does."

His eyes locked with hers as he stopped touching her hair. "You gave me your energy. Your life force."

"Yes."

"As I said, it's complicated."

"Will-"

"Abby, we're running out of time."

The realization hit Abby that he was right. She hopped off the bed to grab her traveling case. "Yes, we must leave before Frederick comes back."

Will grabbed her arm before she could get very far. "There is something else I would rather do."

His cheeks pinked with his quiet words. Abby gazed at him in confusion.

"Abby, do you take me as your husband?"

"What are you talking about?"

"Abby, I take you as my wife, to have and to hold 'til death do us part."

His voice was deep, soft, and gentle. In her chest, Abby could feel the love radiating from him. His eyes watched her, waiting for her to reciprocate.

"Will, I take you as my husband, to have and to hold 'til death do us part."

Will's smile was sweet as he stepped closer to her and took her hand. "I wish I had bought your ring, but that was to be something that I purchased with my earnings when I returned. No bother. I love you, Abby, with all my heart and soul."

"I love you, too, Will. But I don't understand what we are doing."

Will glanced at the bed with a mischievous look on his face. "It's a shame we never got to christen our marriage bed."

Abby snorted, and Will's eyes snapped back to look at her. "I say we christened it plenty a few days ago."

"That's a sharp tongue in your head. Maybe I should put it to better use." His fingers traced the edge of her chemise where it met her skin. "And to correct your words: *you* christened it. I was a spirit and unable to contribute."

Abby gave a short laugh. "I think you contributed enough." She eyed him suspiciously. "Honestly, Will. What are you talking about?"

Will stood taller. "I declare this our wedding night. We said our vows in the sight of God and creation. I want to love you like we were always meant to be."

Abby cocked an eyebrow at him. "Our wedding night?"

Will grinned as he pulled her close. "That's right." His fingers caressed her cheek, moving down her neck to the collar of her chemise. His brown eyes sought out her green ones. "Tell me that you want me to make love to you."

Goosebumps erupted across her skin as his fingers skimmed down to rest at her sternum, waiting for her answer. His thumb rubbed the boning of her bodice.

Abby swallowed. Her nerves were aflame; a ridiculous notion, since Will had already seen her naked and wanting. She nodded and said softly, "Yes, I want you to make love to me. Very much."

Will eagerly began undoing the clasps of her bodice until it fell away. The hook for her skirt was easy to manage, and the fabric joined the bodice on the floor. Her petticoats quickly joined the rest before Abby held out her hand, and Will helped her step out of the bundle of fabrics. She turned, pulling her hair to the side to reveal the laces of her corset to him. She watched his face as his thick fingers made quick work of removing the corset from her body.

Will leaned down to kiss the nape of her neck sweetly as his fingers delicately pushed the shoulder of her chemise down her arm. His lips left a blazing trail of desire across her shoulder and up her neck. An insistent pulse of want gathered in her stomach. Will's nose nuzzled her hair as his arms wrapped around her waist, pulling her even closer.

It was almost too much as Abby turned to him and pushed his suspenders off his shoulders. A swirl of emotions whirled through her head when he bent down to catch her lips in a kiss, but she maintained her senses enough to pull his shirt out of his pants. Will broke the kiss to grab the back of his shirt and tug it over his head. The offending fabric fell from his grasp onto the floor, joining her clothes.

Abby's breath caught in her lungs at the sight of his sculpted chest and stomach. Her fingers grazed the ridges and rises of his muscles, wandering his exposed skin. Will kissed her forehead. A light press to her temple. Lips grazing her cheek. Abby's fingers made their way up his neck to his face.

"Like what you see?" he teased as he smiled.

Abby nodded and blushed. She remembered when she saw him without his shirt as he chopped wood for the stove, or when he was building the furniture for the cottage. How Abby had wanted to touch him then but was never permitted. But now, no one was going to tell her she couldn't. She pulled him to her, and they kissed again as Will pushed her chemise over her shoulders, letting it pool onto the floor at her feet.

Will gazed with awe at her nakedness, and her blush deepened, spreading down to her chest.

"I still can't get over how beautiful you are," he muttered as he kissed her again. His hand brushed down her neck to her chest before cupping one of her breasts. Will marveled as he watched his hand completely engulf it, sighing when his thumb grazed her nipple, which perked to attention. "Absolute perfection."

Abby scoffed at his words, and he gave her a scolding look.

"I always wondered if your freckles were everywhere," Will mused as he caressed her curves and dips while expressing his devotion and adoration. "Now, I know they are. Thank goodness because I can't wait to kiss every one of them."

Each of his touches sent tingles across her skin, electrical pulses that left goosebumps in their wake. While Will's touches in his spectral form had brought her to bliss quickly, these touches were soft and intimate, like teasing kisses on her skin. Abby couldn't get over how big his hands looked on her body, and how little her hands looked on his.

Will led her to the bed and bid her to lie down as he followed her. His body hovered over her as he blessed her skin with kisses and caresses that ignited a simmering fire in the pit of her stomach. The apex of her thighs ached for more of his attention there, as Will tantalized her lower abdomen and thighs with his touch. He smiled into her skin between kisses as she growled at him when he teased the soft curls on her quim before cupping her breast again.

"Will," she whined. "Please."

Her body sang with need when his fingers made contact with her folds.

"So wet," he growled. "Do you need me, my love?"

"Yes, please, Will," Abby begged.

He kissed her deeply as his fingers moved through the

wetness at her apex, finding a special nub that he gave special attention. Her breath hitched as he swirled his finger on that place while he kissed down her neck. Abby bucked under him and found herself breathless as he continued to play with her. She clung to his arms, desperate for an anchor as his touches made her feel like she was drifting away to the stars high in the night sky.

A coil deep within her continued to tighten when one of his thick fingers pressed into her entrance. He broke his biting kiss that he was working on the apex of her neck, groaning into her skin about how tight she was. His finger worked her in and out as he proceeded to swirl his thumb on her bud. He added a second finger as he thrust in and out of her tight space. Her nails dug into his skin as her back began to arch. A roaring wave of pleasure rolled through her body, the coil deep within her snapping, drowning her in sweet bliss as she called out his name.

His fingers quickly left her as he scrambled off the bed, and she mourned the loss of his touch. She watched as his fingers fumbled to find the closure of his pants. Shakily the buttons were undone, and his pants fell to the ground, leaving his erect manhood displayed. Abby couldn't help but stare as he climbed on the bed again. She studied curiously how Will pumped his erection a few times, a smirk on his lips. It was large and long, standing tall in a bed of dark blonde curls as it curved to his belly.

Abby swallowed hard as she watched him come closer to kneel between her thighs. She had heard the talk amongst the married women at the dock who gossiped while cleaning the fish for market. But here, as she gazed at her first cock, she became very unsure of what they were doing. Abby felt her body flush with embarrassment as Will caressed her thigh from her knees up to her hips, sliding her closer to him.

She couldn't meet his intense gaze as he rubbed his length through her glistening folds.

Will's finger hooked under her chin, bringing her eyes to meet his. "Do you still want me?"

His question was tender and vulnerable, like he was afraid of her rejection. Abby surely wanted him, but was worried about disappointing him.

"Yes," she breathed.

Will kissed her tenderly, his lips moving sweetly over hers as she felt him pressing his length into her entrance. He was slow and steady as he burrowed into her. Abby broke their kiss as she tried to catch her breath, her fingers digging into his biceps as his body overwhelmed her. Will's breathing was uneven and sounded a touch pained. Abby felt a slight discomfort within her channel as her body gave way to accepting him. About halfway in, her body relaxed enough to open, and his shaft quickly filled her, pushing the air out of her lungs.

Will breathed heavily, pressing his forehead to hers as they took a moment to revel in the feel of the connection.

"Are you well? Did I hurt you?"

Abby bit her bottom lip to hold back her nerves while she shook her head. She had never imagined she had been so empty before, but now he filled her so perfectly. Will took a deep breath and released it slowly.

"I'm going to move now," he murmured and pulled out a small amount before filling her again.

Abby gasped at the sensation. His strokes became longer, and Will groaned. Abby's discomfort bloomed into a delicious slide of his length that took her breath away over and over. Will devoured her lips, plunging his tongue into her mouth. His tongue caressed hers as he swallowed her moans. Her desire rose, teeming with a passion that made her stomach swoop.

His hand caressed every part that he could reach as he supported himself with the other. His lips brushed her skin and painted it with colors that bloomed as he sucked, bit, and kissed her skin, marking her as his. Will breathed words of perfection and beauty into her skin, and they seeped into her pores, never to leave. He used words and phrases like 'mine,' 'so tight,' and 'warm and welcoming' as each thrust buried deep inside her.

Abby didn't know that sex could feel like this, such a strong deep connection that she could almost sense him everywhere, especially in her soul. She wrapped her legs around his hips, changing the angle so he hit deeper, and they both groaned. Will grabbed her hip to hold her closer to him as he slammed his hips faster into her. He pulled such sounds from her body and mouth, and Will's thumb found its way to her nub at her apex again, swirling.

Abby's muscles started fluttering around his length, and her eyes opened wide in wonder as she stared at his face. She clawed at his arms and shoulder, trying to find a place to hold onto as her heart raced so fast that she couldn't catch her breath. It felt almost like a panic deep within her, building and growing as his thumb flicked and swirled, and his thrusts increased in speed.

It was like a chase, but what they were chasing, Abby wasn't sure. It was similar to when Will touched her in his phantom form – a build and release, but this was definitely different and more intense. Her body tensed and released, only to repeat as he moved.

Just as she didn't think she could feel a more powerful feeling than the moment before, an exquisite fire of ecstasy burned through her as her orgasm sang through her veins, dissolving her into pleasure as she moaned out Will's name. Will's breath hitched as her muscles gripped his cock. His rhythm stuttered for a moment as he slammed faster into her.

Will groaned and moaned as he urgently chased his pleasure. Her name fell from his lips repeatedly as she shivered in his arms. Abby's fingers brushed his hair as she watched his face in her bliss. His eyes were wild in hunger and desire, with his hair tousled and sweaty. Will grunted loudly as his length pulsed deep inside her, and warmth spread from his spend. He made a few more short thrusts before he shuddered over her with his eyes tightly shut, his nose scrunched, and his mouth wide in surprise.

Will panted heavily as he studied her euphoric expression. Abby hummed and sighed in her happiness as she pushed a strand of his hair behind his ear. He kissed her, and she welcomed him, her fingers curling into his hair.

He pulled away to gaze into her eyes. Abby saw the raw emotion behind his eyes that echoed in her heart. She wanted to say so much, but there were not enough words to describe everything she felt in her heart and soul. Instead, she kept her words simple as she placed all her emotions into them.

"I love you, Will."

His fingers pushed the hair off her face, and she pulled him down to kiss her again. Abby wanted to crawl inside him so he could never leave her, or hold him tightly to anchor him to the Earth. She would fight anyone or anything that tried to take him from her again.

He pulled his softening cock out of her body, and she winced a little in discomfort, but she didn't mind it. It was like he left an imprint of himself inside her that she could still feel. As he lay next to her, she curled into his body, her head resting on his chest, listening to his racing heart as it began to calm.

Abby's finger carded through a small patch of blonde hair at the center of Will's chest as his arms pulled her tightly to his body.

"You're my everything, Abby."

She glanced up at him as he smiled down at her. Abby cupped his face, her thumb rubbing his skin delicately. She pushed her body up so her face was hovering in front of his. Her eyes roamed over his face until they rested on his beautiful, soulful eyes. She silently blessed and thanked every deity and fae and spirit for this moment with him; for answering her prayers and pleas.

Will rubbed her back with one of his hands, soothing her while caressing her bottom with the other. Her hair cascaded around their faces like a curtain, hiding them from the reality that settled around them.

This moment was not forever. Abby couldn't freeze time and savor it forever.

His eyes wandered over her face before landing on her lips. Abby moved in for a kiss, but before their lips connected, Will whispered, "I love you."

Then he lifted his head to catch her lips. Abby's heart soared as he rolled them over, slotting his body between her thighs again. She could feel his cock hardening against her leg as they continued to kiss. She wanted to bottle up this feeling of bliss and desire and keep it with her always. Their bodies intertwined, and when he slid home deep within her once more, she welcomed this passionate seduction with a fiery yearning.

11

Wanton Satisfaction

For hours, they made love between bouts of holding each other tenderly. Abby curled into Will's body as her head rested on his chest. His hand rested on her hip and buttocks, his thumb grazing her hip bone. Will gazed into her eyes with such love that Abby felt like the world had stopped.

"I loved you from the first moment I laid eyes on you," he murmured as she rubbed his back. "Your face set in a scowl as you walked down the pier with your reddish-gold spun hair braided neatly in a bun. You had a lock that had broken free, curling into your face to your utmost annoyance as you kept sweeping it away with the back of your hand. Your green eyes were like the turbulent ocean, stormy and full of dangerous promise."

Abby listened to his heartbeat, and he took a deep breath, releasing it with a sigh. "You talk about me like I was this thing of beauty."

Will smiled at her. "You were to me, especially after you called me a hulking ox for being in your way. It was then, as you passed by in all your fiery indignation, I turned to Frederick and Edward and declared my intentions to marry you one day."

Abby snorted a laugh. "My insulting you made you fall in love with me?"

"Aye. It was your spirit that drew me to you. Not some demure flower or submissive, but a match for me. I never wanted simple love. I wanted a woman to challenge me and love me with all the fire of passion."

They lay there, lost in thoughts of the past. Abby couldn't help but regret that they hadn't acted sooner. That they had waited too long to marry. Would the events of ten years ago have happened if they had wed earlier?

He kissed her on the forehead as he shifted his body to lay her on her back. "I need to taste you again," he cooed as he took in her confusion.

He kissed down her body, paying particular attention to her breasts as he passed before nestling himself between her thighs like he had done several times already. Abby gasped at the sensation as his tongue passed through her folds. Her hand made its way into his mussed hair, scratching his scalp. Will groaned into her quim wantonly at her touch, his large hand pressing her stomach to keep her right where he wanted her.

Abby couldn't help but think they had been robbed of these moments by his death. Even though they had been granted this moment, she couldn't help but feel they were on borrowed time.

Abby cried out his name as his glorious tongue and talented fingers brought her to ecstasy once more, and tears broke free from her eyes at the unfairness of it all. Will's smile fell as he took in her tears and gathered her into his arms.

"My love, did I hurt you?"

Abby shook her head. "No, you did not."

His thumb brushed the tears from her cheek. "Then why do you cry?"

"It's not fair. We should have had this all along. Why did you have to be taken from me in that terrible storm? I know it was an accident and that the waves were strong, but-"

Will placed a finger on her mouth. His lips were set in a grim line as his eyes studied her face. "Who told you it was an accident?"

The intense danger in his voice startled her. "People on board the boat."

"Who?" he demanded.

"Edward was one."

Will nodded as if accepting her answer as a reasonable one. "You said he was one. Were there others?"

Abby nodded. "Yes, Frederick told me. In fact, he was the first to inform me of your death. Of course, I refused to believe -"

Abby stopped her words when she saw a great fury in his eyes.

"Frederick."

"Yes."

Will pulled away from her and sat up, his hands carding through his hair. Abby sat next to him and placed a hand on his back.

"What is wrong?"

"How did Frederick say I died?"

He turned to watch her face. Abby furrowed her brows. "Well, he told me you fell overboard during a great wave, and they could not find you."

Will waited for her to add more, but Abby didn't have any. He turned away from her again in silence.

"Well, Edward told me a bit more -"

"Edward was on the other side of the boat," Will snapped. "He did not see what happened."

Will stood to get away from her touch. Abby watched as he paced the floor.

"I wondered when I felt your betrayal in my slumber why you would promise yourself to a man like Frederick Evans." His voice was biting and angry. "My spirit awoke and sought you out to remind you of the promises you made to me."

"Promises?"

Will turned sharply to watch her expression. "To honor me and my memory. Day after day I listened as you stood upon the shore. I heard your vows to be true to me if I would only come back to you."

"But you didn't come back. I waited almost ten years for your return. I prayed to every deity and fae known to man. I tried to bargain with God for your safe return. I was faithful to you all that time!" she hissed at him.

"I tried to come back. I always did, but the sleep had too strong a hold on me, keeping me down in the depths of the ocean, slumbering and waiting."

Abby eyed him curiously. She was almost afraid to ask. To speak the words she knew he wanted her to ask him. "For what?"

"For my revenge."

His words stunned her. She could only stare at him as he studied her, gauging her reactions.

"Revenge against whom?"

"My murderer."

Abby blinked up at him as her mind drew a blank. He was murdered? But that didn't seem right. Who on board that ship would want to murder him?

"I don't understand."

Will huffed in frustration as he resumed his pacing. "What did Edward tell you of that day?"

"That the storm came out of nowhere and caught you all by surprise. You were lashing the equipment to the deck. Billy washed overboard, and then Archie. You tried to save Archie and were knocked overboard, your hand catching the railing. Frederick freed himself of his bindings to help you, but you were weighed down. The rope holding you broke, and you fell."

Abby thought about her words, but none of what Will was saying made sense. Frederick was the only one near him to cause harm, but Frederick and Will were like brothers. Frederick would have never hurt Will.

Will sat next to her on the bed, and his expression softened. "What Edward told you was what he would have seen, which is the truth from his point of view. But that is not all that happened."

Fear gripped Abby's heart. Her mind almost didn't want to know what he was about to say, but she braced herself. Will cupped her face tenderly and kissed her.

"What truly happened, Will? I am so frightened to know, but I must understand."

Will sighed heavily. "Archie did go overboard, and I was able to grab his hand. I was pulling him up when a large wave washed over us, pulling me over the railing. My rope held, but the line securing a crab trap to the boat wrapped around my leg along with a cable with a couple of empty baskets.

With my free hand, I was able to grab the railing, but the wave pulled Archie from my grasp. Frederick did rush to the rail to try to pull me up at first. Then, I saw his expression change from determination to consideration. I yelled for him to hand me a knife so I could cut the rope around my leg free to allow the metal trap to fall into the ocean. He pulled out his knife and stared at it while I begged him to hurry. I could feel the waves catching the trap and tugging on my leg. My hand on the railing was slipping, and I knew I didn't have much time. I prayed the rope would hold me long enough to climb aboard so I could return to you, my love. All I could think of was coming home to you.

Frederick told me he would help me if I would grant him one favor. Something inside me told me to ask about the favor he wanted. So, I did. He asked me to abandon you so he could marry you - my life for your hand. I told him no. He made quick work through most of the line before I could protest. He asked me one last time, and I refused. He finished his cut as another wave hit us. The rope separated, sending Frederick out of my sight onto the boat, and my hand slipped from the railing. I plummeted into the ocean, barely gathering enough breath before I hit the surface.

The waves battered me as I tried to swim to the surface, but the metal trap dragged me down too fast. I turned my efforts to the rope weighing me down, trying to undo the knot, but my fingers went numb from the cold. Soon, I couldn't hold the air in my lungs anymore. I panicked as I tried to swim again. I needed to get home to you. I promised you that I would return. But the air escaped my lungs, and the cold waters of the sea rushed in; all the while, the trap took me to the depths. As my vision clouded, my last thoughts were of your smile and kiss until I was no more."

Abby wept over his words. He held her tightly to his chest as she cried and groaned in misery. Will spoke words of comfort as he wiped the tears from her face. When she finally settled down enough to look into his face, she saw the tears staining his face.

Abby kissed his cheeks, making a path to his lips. She kissed him with such a passion that Will, even in his sadness, returned it with a whimper.

"You are mine," she choked as she pushed Will down onto the bed.

Her lips devoured his, tongue plunging into his mouth to taste him as she straddled his waist. Will grunted as she moved over his length, causing it to firm again. When his erection caught her entrance, she sunk on his cock, enveloping him in her warmth.

Abby broke their kiss with a moan as their hips met. She watched his broken face as she began to move. She wanted to feel anything but the sadness in her heart. Abby wanted him to fill her up with joy, passion, pleasure, and, most of all, his seed.

"I am yours," she purred as she rode his shaft, his hands grasping her hips to urge her on.

Abby loved watching Will's face as the pleasure rolled through him. He looked ruined with each roll of her hips. His hands worshiped her body, cupping her breasts to massaging her bottom, urging her to go faster. She leaned forward to place her hands on his chest, changing the angle of how he hit her deep within her body. Will responded by meeting her thrusts as he moaned her name over and over.

Abby came hard as her body slowed, crying out his name to the heavens so her Will would never be forgotten, and Will rolled them over, pushing her further onto the bed. His thrusts into her pliant body became more desperate and erratic with such speed as he huffed and grunted. Abby smiled as her hand brushed the hair that had fallen into his face away from his eyes.

He watched where their bodies met as his length disappeared over and over inside her. His thumb met her nub and began building her back toward her bliss. Abby grabbed onto his shoulders to brace herself, shattering as a wave of intense pleasure hurtled through her body. She groaned Will's name as she felt his member pulsing deep within her. Will groaned with each release of his seed deep within her womb before he collapsed in exhaustion on top of her.

They panted onto each other's skin as they tried to catch their breath. A thought rolled through Abby's mind that didn't belong there after such bliss, and she wished her fears away to no avail. She couldn't lose him again.

Abby pushed on Will's chest to gaze into his eyes. She tried to blink away the tears that threatened to fall as she attempted to form the words that needed to be said.

"You can't stay, can you?"

Will shook his head in abject misery. "No, I can't. I only absorbed enough of your life force to manifest in this way for only a short period of time, and I dare not take anymore. When the sun rises, I will be a spirit again."

Pure rage rolled through her body. She was angry at the unfairness of having everything she had ever wanted in her grasp– only to have it torn away from her again. Rage at all the years they had lost with each other because of the selfishness of one man.

Frederick.

Brother.

Friend.

Betrothed.

Murderer.

Within all her rage, she found a word that gave her solace in her misery. She at first thought the word was justice, but as the fury began to consume her, she knew it would taste wrong on her tongue. It was a word so profound that her soul sang it to the heavens and the worlds beyond. A word that only she could bring to fruition.

Revenge.

She would have her satisfaction.

12

Confrontation

Abby pushed Will off her and slid off the bed. She grabbed her chemise and threw it over her head.

"Abby, what are you doing?" Will asked in alarm as he stood beside the bed, watching as Abby dug through their clothes to find her skirt.

"I am going to find Frederick. He is not going to get away with your murder."

Will grabbed her arm, making her turn to look at him. "And what do you think you're going to do? Confront him?"

"Maybe. But I'll be damned if Frederick thinks I'm marrying him tomorrow."

Abby pulled her arm out of Will's grasp as she growled at her corset and bodice. There was no way she was going to put those infernal things back on. As she heard movement behind her, she turned to see Will getting dressed, grumbling to himself.

"What do you think you're doing?" Abby spat.

The fire in Will's eyes silenced any other word she was about to say. "You are touched in the head if you think I'm going to let you go alone to confront my murderer."

Will popped his suspenders onto his shoulders as he grabbed his boots. Abby pushed against his chest.

"I just got you back," she whined as her fingers twisted in his shirt.

"Exactly. And you have me until the sun rises. Wherever you go, I go," he grunted as he tied his boots.

Abby growled. "Fine. Frederick can't take on both of us."

Will crossed his arms over his chest as he watched Abby put on her boots. "So, what is the plan?"

Abby snorted. "Plan? Have you really forgotten how I do things?"

Will grunted as he brushed a hand through his hair. "You cannot go in there showing all your cards, Abby. You now know what Frederick is capable of doing. That's why I tried to keep you apart as best I could."

Abby stopped tying her laces to look up at Will. She remembered the times she had been with Frederick since Will's return. Her face darkened as her thoughts landed on one moment in particular. "William Johnson, did you push me on the docks because Frederick touched me?"

Will's eyebrows rose into his hair, and he threw his hands up. "Now, Abby, in my defense, he touched you too intimately and truly –"

Abby turned her ire on him. "I fell! I could've gotten hurt."

Will shrugged at her. "I didn't mean to push you that hard. I tried to comfort you afterward."

Abby finished tying her boot and stood in front of him.

"And the necklace? It just happened to fall on the floor all by itself?"

Will rolled his eyes. "That thing was going to keep you from me. I didn't want it anywhere near you."

Abby shook her head. "There are so many words that come to mind, but I won't say a single one because I am polite."

She grabbed her largest shawl and threw it over her shoulders. Will was staring at her.

"You're going in practically your underclothes to Frederick's house?"

"Seriously, Will. I don't want to struggle with my corset and bodice, all that lacing, and I'm wearing a skirt and shawl. We're going to confront Frederick, break off my engagement, then come home. We'll be back in bed before the moon sinks too far in the night sky."

Abby saw the look that settled in Will's stare – a glimpse of possessiveness that fed the hunger she felt for him deep within her core. Abby knew Will wanted to keep her here to protect her, but they were wasting valuable time arguing. She marched toward the door and out into the dark of night, hearing Will try to keep up with her.

Abby peered over the cliffs to the ocean below until she felt Will touch the small of her back.

"Are you ready to do this?"

Abby turned to gaze into his eyes before she nodded. "We need to confront Frederick. He has gotten away with your murder for too long. He needs to pay for what he has done."

"Then, we do this together," Will said firmly as he took her hand.

They made their way to the narrow path that led down the cliff's face toward town, but as Will crossed the samphire at the edge of the trail, he doubled over in pain. Pain that Abby could almost feel in every fiber of her being. It was like he was being pulled apart from the inside. Will collapsed onto the ground, groaning as she knelt beside him.

"Will, what's wrong, my love?"

Her voice shook in fear as her hands tried to find where the pain was most brutal. He pushed himself away from the path and sighed in relief. Panting, Will looked up at her and took her hands.

"I can't leave the cliff, Abby. We can't go to town."

Abby looked longingly at the few lights left in town before her gaze met Will's. *No, this was not how this was going to end.* Will hadn't even had a chance to confront Frederick with her by his side. They both deserved to tell him that he didn't win. That Will and Abby had found each other again through an act of fate and love, and Frederick could never take that from them. Ever.

"I can go to town," Abby began.

A look of horror crossed Will's face. "No –"

"I will confront Frederick –"

"No, Abby. You can't –"

"Frederick isn't going to get away with your murder."

"Abby," Will pleaded as he gripped her hands tightly, afraid she would slip through his fingers. "He'll kill you. We know he's capable of it."

Abby pulled back far enough to make Will recoil in pain. She had stepped onto the path that he could not follow.

"I have to, Will. Frederick will pay for his crimes. I will make sure."

Tears welled in Will's eyes. "Please, Abby, stay with me until the sun rises. Let us have these precious few moments together before they're no more." His voice cracked. "I don't want to let you go."

"I love you," she whispered as a tear fell down her cheek.

His body tensed as he watched her step farther down the

path.

"No. No. No. No, Abby," he pleaded, his voice broken with his sobs. "Please don't go this way."

"I'm sorry," she breathed before she turned to run down the path.

Her heart broke as she heard his pleas, begging her to return. His cries of misery echoed down the cliff, urging her to move faster. She steeled her resolve, reassuring herself that she was doing this for them. To make Frederick pay for taking the one genuinely perfect and wonderful thing from her life – the love she had with William. With those thoughts, her heart raced, and her feet tried to keep up with the pace as she flew down the path.

As she reached the bottom, she stole a glance back at Will, who stood there in abject misery watching. Her foot touched the road, and a great wail came from the cliffs. It only pushed her faster down the street leading to Frederick's home.

The streets were dark, with only a few glowing lanterns in front of the inn, tavern, and docks. Abby swiftly ran through the empty streets until she came to the porch of the home she was looking for. She stood there for a moment, staring at the familiar door she had gladly come to in the past, seeking Frederick's comfort and friendship. It was a familiarity that had deceived her for so many years.

She marched up to the door and rapped her knuckles hard against the wood. Her knock was met with silence. Glancing around the empty streets, an icy breeze played with the hem of her skirt and the tendrils of her loose hair. She clutched her shawl closer, shivering.

Abby turned and pounded her fist against the wood, hoping it would be enough to rouse Frederick from his slumber. She was rewarded with the creak of wood floors and the shuffle of movement behind the door. Frederick unbolted the locks, and the door swung inward to reveal a sleepy-looking Frederick in a pair of long johns and a dressing robe.

His brows furrowed in confusion as he took in the vision of her standing on his front porch. Abby realized she must have been a sight, her hair disheveled and half-dressed. Frederick's eyes widened in surprise while a cocky grin spread on his mouth. She wished then that she had listened to Will about her appearance. Danger lurked in the space between them. Abby felt the urge to run, to leave that place and fall back into the safety of Will's arms.

"It's freezing, Abigail. Come in and warm yourself by the fire," Frederick insisted as he stepped aside to let her in.

Abby shivered at his words. "No, what I have to say, I can say here."

Frederick's brows disappeared into the dark curls on his forehead. "All right."

"I know what you did."

One of Frederick's neighbors stepped out on the porch, glancing in Frederick's direction. Abby cringed at what this confrontation looked like to the unknowing eye.

"Abigail, I insist you come in before the neighbors start some gossip."

Frederick's hand grabbed her upper arm and pulled her into the house. The door shut behind her as she swiveled to find Frederick crossing his arms over his chest. Abby glanced around the foyer, hearing the fire crackling in the next room. Frederick observed her as she tugged her shawl tighter.

"As you were saying?" Frederick asked as he guarded the door.

Abby's voice shook with every word, and her body vibrated with fear. "I know what you did."

Frederick's expression was like a blank page, void of any emotions. "And what did I supposedly do, Abigail?"

"I know what you did to William."

As soon as Will's name fell from her lips, Frederick turned slightly to the door, and slid the locks into place, the clunk sounding like a nail hammered into a coffin. Abby swallowed hard as Frederick stepped toward her, causing her to step backward.

"And what did I do to Will, may I ask? I was his loyal friend since he started working on the docks with my father. I took care of him."

Each step he took brought Abby further into the sitting room, where the fire mocked her with false hope of welcomed comfort. She would find none in this house, not with the man before her. But that was Abby's fear – that if she stayed, she would never be able to leave.

"No," Abby hissed. "You killed him."

Frederick stopped moving for a moment, his body tense enough that he looked like he was going to pounce on her before he barked a laugh so cruel it caught her by surprise.

"I killed Will? What makes you think that?"

"Because he told me. You cut the rope that held him to the boat and let him fall."

The room held its breath, and the noise of the fire faded as Frederick watched her stumble backward into the back of the sofa. Frederick's face paled, and the corners of his mouth turned downward in displeasure.

"Who told you that? Edward?"

"No, William did."

The quiet fury brewing in his eyes made her question her decisions at that moment. Her eyes flicked to the foyer behind him and the door that meant her freedom. As she concentrated on her escape, Frederick lunged and grabbed her, the shawl torn away from her body as he dragged her to the couch, pushing her to sit down.

Frederick brushed his hands through his hair as he panted, his hands shaking in either fear or anger. Either one was dangerous, and Abby regretted her stubborn-headed behavior. She should have listened to Will, but she did everything Will asked her not to do – showed all her cards. Trapped herself under the watchful gaze of Frederick.

His dark eyes burned as they traced her revealed form, the laces loose on the bib of her chemise, and her hem hiked up on her skirt, showing more chest or leg than she ever wanted Frederick to see. She clutched the fabric at her chest with one hand as she tried to push the wool of her skirt over her leg with the other.

"What are you doing here, Abigail?" Frederick growled. "Coming to my house in the dead of night dressed like some harlot and accusing me of murder?" Abby tried to get up to put some distance between them, but Frederick pushed her back onto the sofa, towering over her. "What are you really here for, Abigail? Do you want our wedding night this evening?"

Fear gripped her heart as his knee made contact with the cushion beside her. Abby wanted William to be here to protect her. She wished she had fled after Frederick didn't answer the door at her first knock. She should have never left that warm nest of a bed, nuzzled in Will's arms.

"Because I don't have a problem with that," Frederick murmured as his hand caressed her leg. He moaned as his fingers met the softness of her skin, pushing up the hem of her skirt. "But to accuse me of murder?" He tsked as he squeezed the muscle of her calf, and she whimpered at the pain.

Abby could hardly breathe as his hand moved up her leg. She cringed at his touch and tried to flee, pushing while attempting to free herself from his grasp. Frederick pulled her back, and Abby kicked at him, trying to knock him away. She needed to distract him so she could leave, but his body was so close that she could smell the soap he used for shaving. Her mind raced to delay his actions, and the words tumbled out of her before she could curb her tongue.

"You murdered my Will in cold blood after you told him you would spare his life if he gave up on me." Frederick's eyes widened as she spoke. "For him to step aside so you could court me. And when he told you no, you cut his rope with your knife and let him fall into the ocean to die," she snarled as she pushed him off her.

Her feet met the floor as she ran for the door while Frederick sat there with a stunned expression, watching her flee. Her shaking hands found the bolts, unlocked them, and threw the door open. The chill of the evening air hit her as she ran across the porch only to have Frederick grab her arm. A cry of surprise escaped her lips, and he pulled her sharply into his chest.

"Release me!" Abby screamed as her arm and legs flailed in panic. She needed to be anywhere but trapped in Frederick's arms. More importantly, she needed to run to the cliffs to find Will.

Lights from the neighboring homes flickered on as Frederick tried to hold on to her.

"Where did you hear that?" Frederick hissed at her. "Who told you that?"

"William told me everything!" she rasped. "He told me everything after taking my maidenhead, claiming me for his own."

Frederick studied her, confused. His grip tightened on her as his face contorted with fury.

"You will never have me," Abby balked. "I am Will's, and he is mine. We are bound in our promises and my blood."

"You lie!" Frederick screamed at her. "He's dead! I killed him because he took you from me!"

Abby laughed in his face. "You can't have what was never yours in the first place!"

Abby's knee connected with Frederick's groin, and he doubled over in pain, releasing her. She then glanced around the street, seeing people on their porches watching the scene before them. Why were they just standing there watching? Why were they doing nothing to help her?

"You bitch!" Frederick growled as he lunged at her.

Abby jumped out of his reach and ran for the cliffs. She heard a woman call her name, but she couldn't stop. Her heart raced as she ran, begging her to grow wings to fly. Abby could hear Frederick behind her, cursing her name.

Distant thunder rumbled, and Abby glanced at the sky; the clouds began covering the full moon. Lighting flashed as she climbed the path toward Will's shadow far above her, looking down. She called to him, yet she knew he could do nothing but watch as the man who killed him chased his beloved up the cliffside.

Abby had to get to Will. Her body ached, and her lungs burned with effort as she climbed. Her only thought was of Will as one step fell after another. Then the rain came, and with it, the voice of Frederick. She turned, shivering in the icy downpour, to the sight of Frederick standing behind her with the glint of a knife in his hand and a wild look in his eyes.

13

Haunted

Abby's panicked heart thudded as she stared down the hill at Frederick. He had a desperate look in his eyes, one that betrayed his intention – Abby would not live another day. She knew too much and felt too little for him, which was a deadly combination.

A flash of lightning and a roar of thunder broke her out of her panic as she turned to rush up the path. Rain poured down onto her, and her linen shift clung to her body as she struggled to keep her footing up the steep hill. The wool of her skirt grew heavy with water as it frustratingly caught on the thorny bushes and weeds lining the path, while the rain threatened to wash away the dirt on the now muddy, narrow trail.

The sea mist descended on her, making it hard for Abby to discern the edge of the path. She could hear Frederick struggling up the trail in his bare feet behind her.

Abby could make out the dark outline of Will standing on the cliff, and she called out to him. "Will!"

"Abby! Hurry!"

She cried out as one of her feet slipped, but Abby caught

herself on a stone to keep herself from falling over the edge, a thorn ripping into her skin. She glanced back through the rain to see Frederick was gaining on her.

"Come on, Abigail," Frederick mocked. "Let's talk about this. We can come to a truce."

Abby laughed as she clambered to her feet. "There is nothing for you to bargain with, Frederick!"

"Yes, there is," he shouted over the howl of the wind as he stalked her. "Your life."

"And we know how well that turned out for William!"

Abby turned and ran the rest of the way up the trail, hearing Frederick's curses as he tried to grab her. A massive shadow in the mist faded, revealing Will standing there, soaked, with his arms opened wide to embrace her. He hugged her quickly before he attempted to pull her away from the edge of the cliff, but Frederick tackled her away from Will's grasp, hauling her up onto her feet.

"You think you can humiliate me? Taunt me?" Frederick growled as his eyes raked over her drenched body, her linen shift keeping nothing hidden from his eyes. "I can take what I want, and no one can stop me!"

Frederick's lips were on hers as she fought against his hold on her. Abby bit down on his bottom lip, tasting the metallic tinge of his blood in her mouth. He yelled in pain, pushing her down. Abby hit the edge of the cliff as she tried to find escape, and Frederick wiped the blood off with his hand, though the rain washed it away. He stood over her, fuming.

"Fucking bitch!" he growled. "You will learn your manners and place."

A large hand grabbed Frederick by the arm and wrenched him away from Abby, roughly. Will loomed over Frederick with fury burning in his eyes.

"If anyone needs to learn their place, it's you," Will hissed. "Get behind me, Abby."

Abby scrambled away from the cliff, hiding behind William. She watched as Frederick's confused expression turned to awe.

"William?" Frederick whispered.

The man looked like he was trying to understand if he was dreaming or if it was real. Frederick reached out and touched Will on the face. Frederick seemed broken, with a haunted expression.

"Aye," Will said, "it's me, *friend*."

Tears mixed with the rain on Frederick's face, sobs rattling in his chest as he gasped for air. Abby watched him, curious about this outburst. Will kept his hold on Frederick firm, but even Will couldn't bear the broken man in front of him. He released Frederick, and Will watched as Frederick collapsed to the ground before them. Abby felt Will's arms wrap around her, enveloping her in a feeling of safety that she craved.

"Are you okay, Abby?" Will asked as he tilted her chin up to gaze into her eyes.

She nodded, blinking the rain out of her eyes, and Frederick laughed maniacally.

Will and Abby turned their attention back to Frederick as he sat on the ground watching them.

"This is some fevered dream!" Frederick said as he stood. "It's not like I haven't seen your face every day since I cut that rope, William! I saw you in the crowd at the dock. In church. Watching me as I walked down the road. And Abigail couldn't shut up about you! Always had to bring you up like you were some saint!" Frederick ran his hands through his wet hair, only to grip it hard and growl. He pointed at Will accusatorily.

"You've haunted me. Tortured me. I thought by getting rid of you, I would finally get everything I wanted."

"How did that work out for you, Frederick?" Will asked as he gripped Abby closer to him.

Frederick shrugged and gestured to Abby. "I couldn't even make her love me! William, you made us both haunted souls drifting at sea with your memory. Both of us unable to shake the thought of you from our minds."

"You took my heart away from me when you cut that rope," Abby snarled. "But you will never have me, Frederick. I have always been William's from the moment we saw each other."

"But he's not real, Abigail! He's a figment of our imagination, a fevered vision of the past!"

Abby stepped forward to stare at Frederick as Will tried to keep her away from him. She shook off Will's hand and stepped into Frederick's space, crowding him.

"No, Frederick. Will lives, and I have married him. I will never be your bride, and you will never take me to your marriage bed. I am completely Will's."

Abby glanced back at Will lovingly, hoping for his reassurance. His gaze told her everything she needed to know: Will's promise to love her forever would never be broken.

Frederick's dark expression turned to horror. His face contorted in raw fury as he snatched Abby, a cry of surprise springing from her lips. She slipped through Will's fingers as Frederick pressed the sharp blade of his knife to her throat. Frederick's hands trembled with a mix of fright and fury, and she shrieked Will's name in despair. She flinched as the blade tasted her blood, holding her breath, fearing a deeper cut if she tried to move anymore. She felt the drop of her life's blood roll down her neck before mixing with the rain.

"You defiled her?" Frederick raged at Will. "Made her your whore? You couldn't leave anything for me, could you?"

Will tried to move to take Abby from Frederick's grasp, but the knife pressed harder against her throat as she gasped. "I took what was rightfully given to me, Frederick. She is my wife in the eyes of God."

"Blasphemist! Defiler! Thief!" Frederick roared. "You can't do any of those things. I killed you! You're dead!"

Will lunged at Frederick, a crackle of ghostly energy radiating from his earthly body, cold and unforgiving as the power of the ocean. Frederick stepped back, teetering precariously near the cliff's edge while dragging Abby with him.

"You're right about one thing, Frederick," Will said lowly, his voice rumbling like the thunder of the storm. "I'm dead."

Frederick studied Will for a moment before breaking out into laughter. "I should add 'liar' to my list of accusations."

Abby watched as Will's eyes began to glow with golden brown light, just like the night on the cliff when she first saw him. Frederick's body tensed behind her as he started to tremble in fear, a whimper escaping his lips. Frederick's arm and hand relaxed their grip on her.

The mist gathered around Will, caressing his body. He reached out toward her and ripped her from Frederick's grasp. Abby fell out of the way as Will advanced on Frederick. Will's presence had an ethereal nature that even affected the weather. The rain bent about him like it feared his touch.

Frederick stabbed his knife at Will in desperation, but the blade passed through Will as if he was the air itself. Frederick made a noise of terror as he stepped away from Will. Abby could see that Frederick wanted to flee, but he had nowhere to go.

"Give in, Frederick, and admit defeat. I will give you the same choice you gave me: Give up on Abby because she is mine, or you will be left to the elements," Will growled, his voice reverberating in the space between them.

"You can't be real," Frederick mumbled as his foot slipped on the muddy ground, bringing him closer to the edge. The knife fell from his hands, embedding it in the softened earth.

Will's form changed into a horrible spectre, glowing with power and rage and lifting him off the ground. Frederick screamed as he stumbled backward, forgetting the cliff behind him. His body seemed suspended for a frightening moment, his face frozen in horror as he realized what was happening, before he fell to the rocks below.

Abby scrambled to the cliff's edge to gaze down at the fallen man as Will's form settled back into his true self. Frederick's body lay unmoving and broken far below, lines of blood coming from every orifice before being washed away by the fading rainstorm.

Will gazed down at Frederick's broken body in sadness and hollow victory, reaching to comfort Abby as she cried.

14

A Fond Farewell

Will scooped Abby into his arms as the clouds pulled away from the full moon, bathing them in its ethereal light. Abby shivered, cradled in his embrace as he made his way into the cottage, placing her in a chair at the table and hurrying to the stove to light the kindling.

"Let's get you out of those wet clothes, Abby," he muttered as he pulled her soaked shift over her head, draping the soggy material over another chair while allowing the saturated woolen skirt to rest on the floor.

After tugging her boots off, Will grabbed a blanket off the bed and wrapped it around Abby's shoulders. Abby could already feel the heat from the stove as its warmth spread throughout the cottage. Will peeled off his wet clothes and boots before grabbing Abby and taking her to the bed. He pulled as many blankets as he could find over them.

She hummed her pleasure at his hands rubbing against her skin, and the warmth of his large body enveloping her. Her shivers slowly dissipated, but the horror of the evening stayed with her.

Frederick was gone. Dead. And she had some part in it, even if she didn't push him over the cliff. It was her actions that brought them to that point.

"It's all over, isn't it?" she whispered into Will's chest as she listened to his heartbeat. A heartbeat that, come morning, would be no more. Abby's heart squeezed in her sorrow.

"Yes," he murmured as his nose nuzzled against her hair. "You don't have to worry about Frederick. He can't hurt you anymore."

"And I'm still going to lose you."

She could feel his nod as Abby turned to gaze into his eyes. The sadness she found there echoed in her soul.

"What if I refused to let you go?"

Will sighed as he cupped her face. "I will fade at morning's light whether you wish it or not. My time here was always fleeting, Abby. My soul belongs within another void that you cannot see or hear."

Abby felt a tear fall down her cheek, and he smiled sweetly at her while wiping it away with his thumb.

"Are you happy there?"

Abby watched as Will thought a moment about her question. "I just am. I feel neither happy nor sad. I exist in that void." He kissed her lips. "But I think of you all the time, and in those moments, I am as I should be – happy."

"Please stay, Will. Make a deal. Plead with the powers that be," Abby begged as her finger laced into his soft hair. "Please don't leave me again. I can't bear to lose you once more."

Will's eyes gazed at her, searching. "Abby, I need you to live your life. To have a family of your own, just like we talked about. Please." His thumbs brushed her cheeks. "I want you to have a full life, my love. For me."

Tears flowed down her face. "There is no life without you, William. You are my life. My happiness. If these few days have shown me anything, you are my joy."

Will sighed as he held her tightly to him. "There is another way."

"Another way?" Abby's heart raced at the thought of them being able to be together.

"You can come with me."

Abby stared at his face. "How?"

His brows furrowed as he tried to find the words. "It's hard to describe. I know you can come with me when I fade away."

At that moment, Abby thought about Sebastian and the rest of her family. About Edward and Sarah. About Myrtle and Emily. They were the people who had supported her in every decision she made. But she had a feeling they might not understand this choice. Letters needed to be written to explain, to justify that she made the right choice by going with Will.

Now though, Will was in her arms, and if these were their final moments together in their true earthly forms before fading into eternity as spirits, Abby was not going to waste a single one of those moments. The emotions that gathered in her breast desired to break free and consume them both. She tugged at Will's hair, dragging his lips onto hers.

Will needed no words to know what she wanted. To be with him one more time before they broke free of their earthly bonds. And as their bodies joined again, their souls sang harmoniously with each thrust and gasp. He devoured each sound that escaped her lips as his hips undulated faster, delving his member deeper within her until Abby felt there was no space between them. No words were left unsaid. They were one mind, heart, body, and soul anchored in their love-making.

When she came, Abby sang his name to the heavens, and he grunted his pleasure with her name on his lips when he found his release. She sighed as he held her in his arms, waiting for their hearts to return to a slow, steady pace.

"We don't have much time, do we?"

Will clung to her. "No, the day approaches. I can feel it."

Abby nodded before she kissed him. She rose to dress, grabbing a fresh chemise, skirt, and bodice. She tossed her corset in disdain as Will laughed.

"At least I will be free from that pain," Abby grumbled as she found paper and a pen to write her letters. And write she did as Will dressed behind her. Abby wrote the words her heart longed to tell the ones she treasured, telling them not to mourn her passing but to celebrate her being reunited with the man she had always meant to marry.

Will brushed his fingers through her hair as he gestured to the window. "We need to hurry to the shoreline."

Abby took a deep breath before she nodded, placing each letter into an envelope. As she stood, Will wrapped a shawl around her shoulders, leaving both their feet bare. With one last look, she gazed upon the home that William had built so lovingly with his own hands. A house that had nurtured her and kept her safe for ten years. A place she was now leaving behind–but not empty-handed. Her hand rested within his, safe and warm, and she was ready to journey with him to their next adventure.

Abby giggled as they ran down the narrow path to the shore, finding that she still enjoyed the soft, cool sand between her toes like she had as a child. She studied Will as he looked out over the ocean, as the waves gently rolled onto the shore. The world was slowly beginning to awaken, just so Will and Abby could say goodbye.

"Miss Abigail!" a voice called over the crash of the waves.

Abby turned to see Myrtle and Emily rushing toward them, lanterns in hand. Myrtle's steps stuttered as she saw William standing beside Abby. Emily glanced curiously at the older woman's reaction–for Myrtle burst into laughter.

"William, my boy! I see you have finally been able to claim your bride."

Will pulled the small woman into a hug. "Aye, Myrtle. I did. And I have decided to forgive your charm." Will shook his head as he tsked her. "Trying to keep me away."

Myrtle shushed him. "It needed to be her choice, William. I was not going to allow you to be selfish."

Emily's eyes widened as she realized what was happening before her. "But he was dead!" the girl murmured excitedly.

Myrtle looked at the girl in amazement. "And he still is. He is just collecting his wife and will be on his way soon."

Abby gave Myrtle a coy smile. "You knew all along, didn't you?"

"That William would never give up, and that he would always return to you? Yes, but the circumstances were a bit vague in my mind."

"Myrtle, I cannot tell you enough how much your help has meant to me. I have left letters at the cottage for you, my brother, and our dear friend, Edward. Please make sure the others receive my farewells."

Myrtle cocked an eyebrow. "And Frederick?"

Abby glanced at Will. "Frederick is dead. He fell from the cliffs, chasing me last night. Myrtle, he murdered–" Abby couldn't continue her words as they caught in her throat.

Myrtle took Abby's hand. "We know. A number of his

neighbors heard his confession of murder last night." Myrtle glanced at Will as he stood behind Abby. "So, he truly murdered our dear William?"

Will nodded. "He wanted me to end my engagement with Abigail. I refused, which resulted in my death."

His answer seemed to satisfy Myrtle's curiosity. The older woman nodded before she gripped Abby's hand firmly. "Are you sure that you wish to follow William? Where he goes, there is no return."

"I meant what I said at your shop, Myrtle. Will is my life. Where he goes, I will follow and be all the happier for it."

"Abby," Will said urgently. "It's time."

Abby quickly hugged the older woman and gave Emily a sweet smile before taking Will's hand. He led her to the shore's edge, where the waves met the sand. He smiled as they stepped into the water until they were thigh-deep. The water was cold and refreshing, invigorating Abby's body with energy. Will pulled her to him, placing a kiss on her lips.

"I love you, Abigail Johnson."

"I love you too, William Johnson." Abby caressed his face with her hand. "Always."

He held her tightly, gazing into her eyes as the first rays of sunlight hit the waves. The light glittered on the water, and Abby felt a tingle growing deep inside her. The outline of Will's form began to sparkle, and Abby felt a lightness consume her until she faded along with Will and was no more.

However, their happiness and love lived on as the foam of the waves and the birdsong in the breeze. It endured and persisted as the sun rose every morning. *Forever.*

15

Not Forgotten

Sebastian Huxley sat in Abby's stone cottage in silence, surrounded by all of Abby's possessions and absorbing the fantastical tale that Myrtle Ravenwood had just relayed to him. He held Abby's letter open in his hand, adorned with the familiar loops of her graceful handwriting sprawled across the page. None of it made sense, and yet –

"So, they just disappeared?" he asked gruffly as he tried to control his emotions. Tears threatened to fall, but he refused to allow them.

Myrtle studied him for a moment. "There are no bodies. They faded into thin air, leaving only the faint trace of laughter in the air."

Sebastian nodded, deep in thought. "And William's murderer? What of him?"

Myrtle poured herself another cup of tea and took a sip. "Frederick Evans paid the price. We found his body at the base of the cliff after that horrible rainstorm. Many people in town heard his confession to Miss Abigail."

How could he not have seen through the mask Evans wore?

Sebastian's guilt tore through him at the thought of arranging a marriage for Abby to the man who murdered William. Abby had told him in her letter that she didn't fault him for the engagement. He simply had not known, just like everyone else in town. Even Abby had never suspected wrongdoing.

Myrtle's hand touched his in comfort. "Do not blame yourself, Mr. Huxley. Miss Abigail had her own mind and made her own decisions."

"That she did." He cleared his throat before continuing. "So, she left me this cottage and all the contents within, but I, for the life of me, have no idea what to do with it."

Myrtle sat back, tugging her shawl closer to her. "I have a young girl, Emily, that works with me. She could act as caretaker of the home and keep it cleaned for when you decide to visit Miss Abigail."

Sebastian's brows furrowed together in confusion. "Visit Abigail?"

Myrtle smiled as her hand swept across the room within the cottage. "Why yes! She and Will are both here, living within these walls and along the shoreline and cliffs." She leaned forward, her finger beckoning him closer to indulge in a secret. "You see, no one is ever truly gone."

Her smile broadened as she stood to take her leave. "Thank you so much for tea."

Sebastian stood and shook her hand. "You're welcome. I will visit you at your shop later with the arrangements for your girl to care for this cottage. I think I will keep it so my wife and I can come to the shore more often."

There was a twinkle in Myrtle's eye when she nodded. "Wise choice. Until later."

With a sweep of her skirts, the older woman left him alone

in the last place his beloved sister called home. There were traces of her and William all over the small space. Embroidered pillows on the bed Sebastian had remembered Abby stitching at one of his visits. The craftsmanship of the chair he sat in that he remembered William using his tools on. He could see the love and care they had each given so tenderly to their home.

Sebastian drank the last of his tepid tea before donning his coat, gloves, and hat. He had paperwork to handle over the estate of his sister. He pocketed the letter addressed to Edward and Sarah Finnigan so that when he met them at the train station, he could deliver it with sad tidings. They had planned to come to a wedding, and now… Sebastian didn't know what to call this event. Abigail's funeral? Her remembrance? Her celebration? He still didn't know exactly what to call it, but he knew he would miss her.

He walked to the end of the cliffs to gaze upon the water. The waves gently rolled in as the breeze played with his red hair. He turned his head at the sound of laughter he heard on the wind - a playful melody that gripped at his heart. A flash of reddish-gold hair out of the corner of his eyes. A movement on the beach.

The image was blurry, like seeing through water, but Sebastian swore he saw a blonde-haired man embracing the lithe figure of a woman with reddish-gold hair. It wasn't until the woman turned that he affirmed it was Abby. She flashed him a bright smile, and the image faded like a mirage.

Sebastian blinked in surprise and wonder, straining to see another vision as the breeze mussed his hair again. He heard a giggle and felt a light touch on his cheek as if a kiss had been placed there. His fingers grazed the place as he looked around the cliffside, hoping for another glance.

"Sebastian," a far-away whisper reached his ears.

"Abby?" Sebastian called softly, his heart wrenching in his chest.

His head pivoted to look at the cottage, and there, faintly, he saw them – William, tall and broad with his arms around Abby, and Abby, her hair loose and free, smiling. He watched as Will turned her in his arms and kissed her before they faded like the morning mist in sunlight.

Sebastian's happiness felt like bursting through his chest, burning away his sorrow. Abby was happy and reunited with her love. What more could he hope for?

He brushed his hand through his hair to straighten it before placing his hat on his head. His path was sure, as well as his mind. As he made his way into town, Sebastian smiled.

No one is ever truly gone.

About the Author

Christina D. Ambrose lives in not always sunny Florida with her husband, three children, three dogs, and a cat. She spends her days writing stories her mind dreams up and her nights hanging out with her hubby, children, and pets until she collapses in exhaustion. She's a huge sci-fi, mystery, and fantasy nerd with a love of reading, movies, theatre, and history. When she's not writing original stories, you can find her writing fanfiction for her favorite fandoms.

You can connect with me on:

- https://www.christinadambrosewriter.com
- https://twitter.com/ChristinaDAmbr4
- https://www.facebook.com/profile.php?id=100085755146556
- https://www.instagram.com/christina.d.ambrose
- https://www.tiktok.com/@authorchristinadambrose

Also by Christina D. Ambrose

The Exception to the Rule

Memoirs of Being an Omega: Book One

Violet Dawson loves her job as an event planner at Hughes Publications. She's spirited, independent, and definitely not your typical Omega. She's determined not to be drawn to the gorgeous Theodore Chamberlin, senior editor and company Alpha asshole. She hates him. Truly she does, even when he smells like heaven on earth.

They are thrust together to plan an event, and all seems to go well until Violet's workspace floods, and they have to share an office.

What will become of them when their close proximity causes Violet to go into heat? Can they put aside the experiences that have made them guard their hearts? Or are their differences too much for them to find true love?

The Exception to the Rule is the first book of the Series, *Memoirs of Being an Omega*, which follows four Omegas - Violet, Rachel, Alex, and Mia - in their quest for true love.

Easier Said Than Done

Memoirs of Being an Omega: Book Two

Rachel Sanders is a hopeless romantic. Truly, she is, but as a spunky and opinionated Omega with a take-charge attitude, she has on many occasions put the fear of God into her share of Alphas, Omegas, and Betas alike as the personal assistant of the CEO of Hughes Publications. Sometimes, that kind of reputation makes it hard to build friendships, let alone romantic ones.

Enter Joseph Lauder, a stubborn-headed Alpha from accounting and Rachel's friend of two years. Nice guy. Handsome in that unconventional way. Red Hair. Freckles galore. Dorky smile. Tall and in dire need of meat on his bones. You know, Rachel's perfect man. She longs for a deeper connection in her relationship with Joseph, but something always seems to get in the way – her job, her exceptional skills at poker, or the fact that Joseph always keeps her at arm's length.

That all changes the moment Joseph asks her in a panic to accompany him on his annual family outing at a ski resort to avoid his parent's meddling. All she has to do is pretend to be his girlfriend for one week.

Getting involved is a terrible idea, and Rachel has half a mind to refuse because she knows this can only lead to one place – heartbreak. But then again, maybe if he sees how good they can be as a couple, all the pieces will fall into place.

She's an Omega on a mission with an infuriating Alpha fake boyfriend and one week to prove they are meant to be. What could go wrong?

Easier Said Than Done is Book Two of the Series *Memoirs of Being an Omega*, which follows four Omegas - Violet, Rachel, Alex, and Mia - in their quest for true love.